I love how Roseanna has cleverly [...] with her brilliant new Christmas [...] So many delightful layers to this tale, along with intriguing characters and beautiful descriptions . . . it really puts you in the mood for Christmas and maybe some sweet sugar plums too!

—Melody Carlson, author of *The Christmas Tree Farm*
and *A Royal Christmas*

Sugar plums, gingerbread, and all the Christmasy feels go into this charming holiday romance penned by reader favorite Roseanna M. White. Escape to an English country manor home where dueling suitors vie for the hand of an earl's daughter. Who will she favor at the Christmas ball? Grab a cup of tea and curl up for a great read to find out!

—Michelle Griep, Christy Award–winning author
of *Once Upon a Dickens Christmas*

Praise for *A Noble Scheme*

"Intrigue, romance, and danger abound in this Edwardian-era tale of two sleuths on a secret mission with entirely different motives. *A Noble Scheme* immerses you in English high society, where little is as it seems and love undergirds everything. Roseanna M. White's second book in THE IMPOSTERS series is as clever as it is glamorous."

—Laura Frantz, Christy Award–winning author
of *The Seamstress of Acadie*

"Two stories are mirrored in Roseanna White's *A Noble Scheme*— the mystery of a missing child and a heartbreakingly tender tale of grief and healing. With characters believable and unique, and a pace that builds suspense as the story unfolds, each thread is so compelling I couldn't stop turning pages."

—Lori Benton, author of *Burning Sky*
and other historical novels

Praise for *A Beautiful Disguise*

"There are few things more joyous than stepping into the pages of a Roseanna White novel. *A Beautiful Disguise* has all of the hallmarks of this beloved author's resplendent fiction: pitch-perfect historical research, a thrilling setting and perfectly paced plot, and a love story that sparks as wonderfully as Lady Marigold's effervescent intelligence and charm. An unputdownable delight by a true master."

—Rachel McMillan, author of *The Mozart Code*
and *Operation Scarlet*

"White's well-woven plot is engaging from start to finish with delightful threads of mystery, romance, and inspiration."

—Carrie Turansky, award-winning author of *No Journey Too Far* and *The Legacy of Longdale Manor*

Books by Roseanna White

LADIES OF THE MANOR
The Lost Heiress
The Reluctant Duchess
A Lady Unrivaled

SHADOWS OVER ENGLAND
A Name Unknown
A Song Unheard
An Hour Unspent

THE CODEBREAKERS
The Number of Love
On Wings of Devotion
A Portrait of Loyalty

Dreams of Savannah

THE SECRETS OF THE ISLES
The Nature of a Lady
To Treasure an Heiress
Worthy of Legend

Yesterday's Tides

THE IMPOSTERS
A Beautiful Disguise
A Noble Scheme

Christmas
AT SUGAR PLUM
MANOR

ROSEANNA M. WHITE

BETHANYHOUSE
a division of Baker Publishing Group
Minneapolis, Minnesota

Published by Bethany House Publishers
Minneapolis, Minnesota
BethanyHouse.com

Bethany House Publishers is a division of
Baker Publishing Group, Grand Rapids, Michigan

Printed in the United States of America

Library of Congress Cataloging-in-Publication Data
Names: White, Roseanna M., author.
Title: Christmas at Sugar Plum Manor / Roseanna M. White.
Description: Minneapolis, Minnesota: Bethany House Publishers, a division of
    Baker Publishing Group, 2024.
Identifiers: LCCN 2024010445 | ISBN 9780764242922 (paper) | ISBN 9780764244056
    (casebound) | ISBN 9781493448159 (ebook)
Subjects: LCGFT: Christian fiction. | Novellas.
Classification: LCC PS3623.H578785 C55 2024 | DDC 813/.6—dc23/eng/20240314
LC record available at https://lccn.loc.gov/2024010445

Scripture quotations are from the King James Version of the Bible.

Cover design by Dan Thornberg

Author is represented by The Steve Laube Agency.

Baker Publishing Group publications use paper produced from sustainable forestry practices and postconsumer waste whenever possible.

24 25 26 27 28 29 30   7 6 5 4 3 2 1

1

19 December 1902
Plumford Manor, Castleton, England

*F*eeling ever so sneaky, Lady Mariah Lyons eased into the bustle of the kitchen, a smile barely contained by her lips. The gramophone she carried was more awkward than heavy, but she was relieved when she could slide it onto one of the few unused surfaces just inside the doorway. Only because of the flurry of impending guests and celebrations could she remain unseen even this long. Usually the moment she stepped foot in the kitchen, someone was trying to shoo her back out again.

Well, not today. She sniffed appreciatively as she adjusted the horn of the record player, ignoring the scents of dinner and bread in favor of the fragrance she waited all summer and autumn to smell: gently baking sugar plums.

The cook's granddaughter caught sight of Mariah, and her blue eyes went as wide as her grin. She dashed over to her side, her head just reaching Mariah's elbow. "My lady!" she whisper-shouted. "Mumma said I was the best snow fairy *ever* in the play."

Grinning, Mariah crouched down, smoothing back the girl's stray curl of hair as she remembered how the little one had spun with more enthusiasm than skill in the little play the village children had put on last Saturday, the script for which Mariah had spent several happy hours on, and the costuming and set design even more. "You were magnificent. And I have a special job for you today, too, Joy."

The little one nodded solemnly, her eyes tracing every plane and curve of the gramophone. Mariah tapped the crank. "Whenever the record begins to slow down, I need you to crank this a few times. All right? Like this." She demonstrated a few quick turns and then let the six-year-old do the same, amidst many giggles. The turntable gained speed and reached its maximum.

"Perfect." Mariah put a finger on the needle arm and grinned. "Ready?"

"Yeah!" Joy bounced up and down on her toes, clapping when the needle touched the record and the first notes of Christmas cheer sang through the room in the form of the opening bars of "God Rest Ye Merry Gentlemen."

Mariah showed her where she'd stashed more Christmas music under the table late last night, to be put to use when they grew tired of that first record. She then shifted her gaze to the rest of the kitchen, the cheer in her own heart increasing threefold as she saw each of the busy staff pause, just for a moment. Their tireless hands took a moment's respite. Their faces moved from harried determination to a remembrance of why they were in such a flurry. Peace, there on Abbie's face. Joy on Mary's. Contentment on Mrs. Trutchen's, as she arranged the dried plums awaiting their first coating of sugar.

Mrs. Trutchen greeted her with a smile. "I wondered where you were, my lady. The first batch is nearly done their first bake."

Mariah sighed. "Mama insisted my hair be properly coiffured, though I don't know why she bothered when she knew very well I'd just come straight down here and let the heat ruin it."

The cook chuckled and passed Mariah a bowl brimming with sugar crystals. "Her ladyship is excited—and rightfully so."

No, her mother was anxious, which was altogether different. Mr. Cyril Lightbourne, presumed heir to her stepfather, the Earl of Castleton, would be joining them at Plumford Manor for the first time in twelve years, and Mama was turning into a regular Mrs. Bennet of Miss Austen fame, muttering that one of her daughters had better win his eye so that the estate could remain in the family.

Mariah picked up a sticky dried plum with her right hand, dropped it into the sugar, and rolled it about with her left, transferring it then to a waiting baking sheet. A process she would repeat hundreds of times before the morning was out, if she had her way. To the cook, she only smiled. "Excitement doesn't explain wasting time on my hair this early in the day."

Mrs. Trutchen chuckled again, her own hand motions the match to Mariah's. It was she who first taught Mariah how to keep both one's hands from becoming a sticky, sugary mess. "And how goes the decorating in the rest of the house?"

Mariah couldn't have held back her smile had she tried. "The transformation from Plumford Manor to Sugar Plum Manor is nearly complete." She punctuated this happy fact with another roll of plums in sugar. Mrs. Trutchen would spend days moving racks from table to oven and back again, rolling and baking each plum at least five times, until what had been a juicy but tart purple treat in the summer became a chewy, sugary delight now. Once they'd finally cooled after their final bake, they'd be portioned into bags of six and tied with a bow.

Then on Christmas Eve would come Mariah's happiest moment of the year. She would stand at Papa's side at the grand entryway to the ballroom and hand a bag filled with sugar plums, marzipan, and a small toy that Professor Skylark had made to each and every child in the region. She'd get to smile and greet each family by name, meet the new children whose parents brought them to the Christmas Eve Ball for the first time, and compliment each parent on the Sunday best they would have donned for the occasion.

Generally speaking, Mariah preferred one-on-one meetings with people rather than crowded ballrooms. But this was the single exception to the rule, because this was a one-on-one greeting of each and every family in her father's earldom—or at least those who were close enough to join them. The only expectation on her was that she be pleasant and welcoming. And even when she went into the ball, she could only dance with her own brother, Papa, the professor, and a few of the neighbors. No one she had to impress. At their holiday ball, unlike every other ball she'd attended, she could just be herself, with no thought of winning the attention of any gentlemen.

Well. Except for this year, of course. But it was only Cyril.

She sighed. Once upon a time, she'd dreamed of him whirling back into her life like the hero of one of her favorite stories. Once upon a time, she'd dreamed of spotting him across a crowded ballroom in London and, with one look from his friendly eyes, finally feeling like she belonged there. Once upon a time, she'd even convinced herself that the fact that his letters had first gone perfunctory and then trickled off altogether would only set the stage for his grand reappearance this Season past, when she was presented at court.

But Cyril hadn't come to London for the Season, only afterward. And according to the gossip mill, he'd taken one look at the most spoiled, cruelhearted, selfish young lady in Town and proven himself no hero in Mariah's eyes. Anyone who gave a second look to Lady Pearl clearly had no sense. No, worse than that—no judgment, and no heart worthy of her admiration.

Which ruled out Cyril and most every other gentleman in England.

But at least she knew it. Knew that Cyril, like everyone else, was the type to be sucked in by shallow beauty and a large dowry. She probably shouldn't even be surprised. Cyril of age ten might have been willing to dream up fantastical worlds with her during his one and only visit to Plumford, but that had been twelve years ago.

What young man would even remember those days with anything but embarrassment?

He probably wouldn't even remember the world they'd created together. *She* might have still loved the old stories so much that she adapted it for the children's play this Christmas, but what were the chances that Cyril would give a whit about Almond Gate or Christmas Wood, Orange Brook or Orgeat Lake?

He would likely blink at her in that way that Fred had perfected, if she dared to mention any of it, and tell her to stop daydreaming.

Her right fingers dropped another dried plum into the sugar, but another sigh sneaked out, slipping into the fragrant air beneath Mrs. Trutchen's hum. She was accustomed to any word of whimsy being met with a frown when she was in the company of society. And yet when she was visiting the sick in the village or helping overburdened mothers with their children, she saw the smiles and joy her stories brought to their faces and hearts. She heard the way the little ones were still running about pretending they were in *her* fairy world. She saw the way everyone in the village went out of their way to greet her and ask her to visit again soon.

Why could her own family never be so glad of her company?

But did the *why* even matter? It was fact. She'd have to learn how to say the right things. To play the role she had no interest in. Accept that whatever man she ended up marrying would likely choose her only because of her dowry and family connections to both the Lyons and Lightbourne estates.

What a dismal future.

Which she wouldn't think about just now. Not at Christmastime. This was the season for joy and miracles, not for the dark clouds of reality. For now, she would simply enjoy the fun and focus on the cheer she'd help to spread to the neighborhood at the ball.

"There you are!" came a relieved voice an hour later.

Mariah startled at her lady's maid's words. She looked toward the doorway to find Blakeley no longer there but rather dodging Joy and the other kitchen workers and, it seemed, every note of

11

the current Christmas carol singing through the room. Her face certainly didn't lighten or brighten as she sidestepped a pan of gingerbread and the maid who carried it.

Mariah had little choice but to frown at her. "What's the matter?"

Blakely's gaze swept over her, and Mariah had the uncomfortable certainty that she noted every strand of hair out of place, every crystal of sugar clinging to her, every wrinkle the apron's tie had given her dress. "Your mother is looking for you, my lady."

As if Mama hadn't known exactly where she would be. It was sugar plum day! This had been her favorite day of the year for as long as she could remember. According to family lore, it had, in fact, been the first day she'd laughed after her mother had married Lord Castleton and moved her three children into his unfamiliar manor house. They said she'd been quiet and shy as a mouse until then, but that Mrs. Trutchen had whisked her away to the kitchens to help with the confections, reasoning that even a four-year-old could roll prunes in sugar, and that she'd transformed after that. Gone from quiet and uncertain to eager to make the place her home and the earl her papa.

Mariah didn't remember that. Just the joy of the tradition and the deep, abiding love for the only father she recalled. But she believed the story. Because something about this day brought back a hint of that first realization of welcome and happiness.

One that Blakely's expression doused with cold water. Mariah reached for the damp washcloth sitting nearby. "What does Mama need me for?"

"The dressmaker is here for your final fitting."

"Already?" Mariah checked her pendant watch—it was only ten o'clock. Mrs. Roy hadn't been scheduled to arrive until after luncheon.

"Your mother sent for her to come earlier. She didn't want to risk you being in your underthings when Mr. Lightbourne arrives."

One of the few points that would have lured Mariah away from her favorite task. Skipping the welcome wasn't optional—much as she almost wished it were—so if she must do it, better not to feel harried. She sent a smile toward Mrs. Trutchen. "I'll return afterward if there's time."

The cook smiled. "We have it in hand if not. Special circumstances, I know."

They were . . . but even so. She'd thought she'd have hours yet to work on the confections. "No help for it, I suppose."

She paused on her way out to praise young Joy's attention to the gramophone. Assured that the kitchen staff would be cheerily serenaded for the rest of the day, she followed Blakely out of the utilitarian, plain-walled portion of the house and back into the elegant and ornate corridors.

Her maid led her directly up the staircase and into Mama's suite of rooms. The sitting room was a flurry of fabric and lace and sequins and beads—enough that Mariah had to pause just inside the door to gape. This was supposed to be a final fitting. Why did it rather look like a dress shop had exploded? "Mama?"

It was her elder sister, rather than their mother, who emerged from Mama's dressing room in a gown of deep red satin and velvet that made Mariah's eyes bulge in appreciation. "Louise! You look stunning."

It was, and had always been, true. Louise was without question the beauty of the family, and it had only deepened after she married Lord Swann and could begin wearing any color gown she pleased. Jewel tones especially complemented her alabaster skin and sable hair.

If only she'd smile once in a while, she'd be without compare. But then, she'd taken her husband's death hard three years ago. Even though her mourning had officially ended well before this last Season, she hadn't felt up to rejoining society. Mariah wondered if she ever would. It had taken Mama ages to convince her to attend the Christmas Eve Ball again this year.

She'd been living at Plumford Manor since a month after her widowhood—the Swann dowager house was still occupied by her former mother-in-law, but her husband's brother had promptly moved into the manor house and made it quite clear she was to vacate the premises. She received her widow's allotment, but having failed to give the family an heir, she had therefore no further claim to the estate.

Poor Louise. She had given her husband both a son and a daughter in their four years of marriage. But neither had lived, and Mariah knew that grief, too, was part of what kept her sister's face in a perpetual mask of ice.

If she didn't let herself feel it, it couldn't destroy her.

Now, Louise glanced down at her gown with a wince. "It's far too ostentatious for a woman of my situation."

"Don't be ridiculous." Mama's voice came from her dressing room, though it was several seconds later that her form followed, voluminous fabric in her arms. "You're only six-and-twenty, darling. Still in your prime, and an honorable widow. There's no reason to assume your life is over."

Louise motioned Mariah forward with the same authority she'd claimed over her all her life, onto the small pedestal Mama kept on hand for fittings. "I assume no such thing. But it is Mariah's turn for attention now."

It was Mariah's turn to wince. "You can have my turn. Really. All those balls . . ."

"I do wish you wouldn't say that, sweetling." Mama draped the gown—that was what the fabric was—over her chaise as the dressmaker emerged from the dressing room, yet more fabric in hand. "And you've never minded this ball, regardless. So chin up, and off with that frock, if you please. You have quite a bit of trying on to do."

Mariah frowned as three more gowns-in-the-making were added to the one she'd already selected—under the careful approval of her mother and sister. "Why?"

"Because the one ball gown won't be enough! You need new dinner gowns as well."

14

"Mama, you outfitted me before the Season. I hardly think—"

"And now it's winter, not summer. Those won't do. You must look your best."

Mariah's frown didn't lessen. "This is an awful lot of fuss over Cyril, isn't it?" Granted, he'd proven himself the sort to be swayed by lovely appearances, if he was paying court to the horrible Lady Pearl Kingeland. But that only proved he didn't deserve the effort—not that he ought to receive more of it.

An opinion her family had never shared.

Mama and Louise both blinked at her for a long moment before Louise blustered out a breath. "Gracious. You weren't with us this morning. I'd forgot."

Funny. She often forgot when Mariah was there.

"You don't know!" Mama spun Mariah around to face the full-length mirror and made quick work of the buttons down her back. "It isn't Mr. Lightbourne we need to impress, Mariah—especially if he's truly all but engaged to Lady Pearl Kingeland, as the latest gossip suggests. It's the greve. He's given up on Lady Pearl and is coming here for Christmas."

"The . . . greve?" She asked it as a question—but it wasn't one. They'd only met one Danish nobleman in the last year, so far as she knew, and the thought of the chiseled-from-ice, too-handsome Lord Søren Gyldenkrone was enough to snatch the breath from her lungs.

When she'd first heard his name, she'd thought it terribly romantic—Gyldenkrone meant "golden crown," after all. And his family was but a step away from the Danish monarchy. Gossip said he'd come to England for the sole purpose of finding an English bride to help solidify Denmark's ties to England, and that he and his cousin, the Crown Prince, already had an agreement that there would be a match between two of their children—which meant whatever woman won his attention would be able to boast a child who was a prince or princess.

Romantic, without question. And he was *so* handsome. She

couldn't help but dream a few dreams when she'd only viewed him from across the ballrooms. But she wasn't like those men who fawned over Lady Pearl—she knew that substance mattered more than form, and the few conversations she'd had with him hadn't resulted in any sort of connection at all. He'd come to pay a perfunctory call twice, yes, but never did she get the impression that he found her charming.

And then *he* had seemingly chosen Lady Pearl as the best option for his bride too—though given how close Lord Kingeland was with King Edward, that made sense. But even so. Couldn't Pearl have left a few suitors for the rest of them?

Which begged the question. "What do you mean? He's coming here?" At her mother's reflected nod, Mariah's hands trembled so that she had to clasp them together. "But why?"

Mama's smile looked more than happy—it looked victorious. "He sent your father a telegram late yesterday, taking him up on the open invitation he'd offered to show him Plumford and the Peak District. And said he was most eager to spend more time with you." Mama leaned in and gave her a swift hug. "You must have made quite an impression on him, sweetling."

Had she? It certainly hadn't seemed like it. He'd cared only about who her brother was, and her stepfather. He hadn't seemed to care who *she* was at all. But then, maybe it was only that he hadn't *shown* it behind that ice-chiseled face.

Maybe there was a speck of hope for an interesting holiday at the manor house after all.

2

*C*yril Lightbourne drummed his fingers against his knee and looked out at the passing landscape less with interest than with a growing worry. It wasn't that the Peak District wasn't lovely—it was, especially with that day-old dusting of snow. It wasn't that he wasn't glad to be escaping London and its freshly minted cruel memories—he couldn't get away from reminders of Lady Pearl soon enough.

It was just that he knew he was about to be a failure. He hadn't been born to be a lord, not really. He wanted only to accept the teaching position at university and talk about literature for the rest of his days. Instead, he would now be under the constant scrutiny of Lord Castleton, who would have expectations Cyril didn't know how to meet. He would have to face the fact that he would stand to inherit this unfamiliar earldom someday, and that the promise of it was the only thing that had opened those doors in London he should have been wise enough not to waltz through.

But as his valet liked to remind him, Cyril had a bad habit of waltzing first and counting the cost later.

It was the fault of those books he read. Far too many stories of romance and adventure and finding friendships in unlikely places.

They'd given him too rosy a view of the world—and of the people in it.

He reached up to touch his fingertips beneath his eye when a twinge fluttered through the flesh, and his valet smirked at him from the opposite bench. "Scarcely noticeable," Kellie said. "I told you it would work."

No doubt it was sour grapes to huff, but he couldn't help himself. "I'm still not convinced it should have. Whoever heard of eating apples and pineapples and red onions to make bruises heal faster?"

"My mum." Kellie's smirk turned to a grin. "And you daren't argue with her. She had plenty of chances to experiment on the lot of us boys, that's for sure, with as many scrapes as we got in when we were lads."

Cyril's lips twitched too. "You say that as if you ever stopped."

Kellie shrugged, no apology in his face—which currently only boasted one cut along his cheekbone, though often it was considerably more. "Fun's fun," he said. "Gotta do something on my half day off."

Laughter rumbled up from Cyril's stomach to his throat. "Most chaps I know would find a book or a girl or even a game of cards—not a fight."

Or a street brawl, from what Cyril could tell. But for whatever convoluted reason, the more bruised and battered Kellie was when he returned from his half day, the happier he was the rest of the week.

Odd duck, that one.

"Most chaps don't know what they're missing. Nothing like a good boxing match."

Cyril shook his head at the comment and probed his eye socket again. "I'm afraid I can't concur."

His valet's gaze went dark under his red brows and face full of freckles. "You're better off. Just remember that."

Academically, Cyril knew he was right. The brawl that had led to the implosion of all his hopes and dreams was to be thanked instead of blamed. It had shown him Lady Pearl's true colors. Or rather, her true feelings—or lack thereof—for him.

Even so, she'd have had to choose another way to let him down if he hadn't shown up to her dinner bruised last week, and it might have been a better way. An easier way. One that hadn't left his ears ringing with her blistering words and his heart more bruised than his eye had been.

And to think he'd earned the black eye defending her honor. But she hadn't wanted to even hear him out on that.

Ah well. In the moment, he'd been glad for the sparring Kellie had convinced him to do, and proud of himself for besting the smart-mouthed Dane who'd been saying things about the lady that no gentleman should have said. And that was still something, wasn't it? Emil Gyldenkrone might think twice before making such claims in the clubs in the future, thinking he could hide behind his brother's pristine reputation. Even if it hadn't impressed Pearl, it could have taught the fellow a lesson. Maybe.

It had taught Cyril one, too, though. One never could trust a pretty young lady's batting eyelashes. He should have known it from the start, but after the way they'd met . . . Well, it should have *meant* something, shouldn't it have? For once in his life he'd gotten to play the hero. He'd read the stories, he knew what that meant—he should have then been *her* hero. The champion always won the princess's hand.

And yet here they were. He might have been twice her champion, but she had no interest in giving him either her hand or her heart, and he was nothing but a fool for having expected it.

He watched the first buildings of Castleton village come into view, noting almost begrudgingly that they were every bit as charming as he remembered from his one and only visit to Plumford Manor twelve years ago.

Kellie let out a low whistle. "Nice little place, isn't it? Looks straight from a postcard."

Cyril grunted his agreement.

Perhaps perceptivity was part of what made Kellie good at his job, but it was also a dratted pain in the posterior now. "You know, it won't hurt you to like it. May even help."

"I do like it. Or did, twelve years ago. But that's the thing." Kellie blinked at him.

Cyril sighed. "I didn't want to then either. My father's whole side of the family is . . ." He made a face, but it was all the explanation Kellie needed. He'd met Mother's people, and it had led to a conversation on the Lightbourne side that Cyril did his best to avoid at all costs. "All cut from the same cloth too. Lord Castleton seemed different, at least to my face."

Leaning across the space between their benches, Kellie studied his face. "You were only a lad. What, ten? Eleven? What did he say behind the back of a boy so young?"

"That I was scarcely related. A stranger. That he couldn't stomach turning everything over to me."

Kellie leaned back again, face contemplative now. "And you're certain that's what he said? That he couldn't stomach turning it over to *you*? Or to a stranger?"

Cyril opened his mouth, shut it again. "Does it matter?"

"Oh, I reckon it does. 'To you' implies he has some argument with you personally. 'To a stranger' means it can be resolved by what you're doing now—becoming *not* a stranger."

The ten-year-old still sulking inside him wasn't willing to grant the point. But the grown man had to do so with a long exhalation and tilt of his head. "You could have pointed that out five years ago."

Kellie snorted. "You hadn't hired me yet."

No. He'd not had the money for a valet until Castleton had granted him an annual stipend upon his twenty-first birthday, just sixteen months ago. He'd granted it with the stipulation that Cyril must report to Plumford Manor for training by the end of 1902 . . . and so here he was. Not because he'd been so eager for the continuation of that income—he'd have lived happily enough on a teacher's salary—but because his mother had threatened to burn his library of books, starting with a book for each day that he went beyond his deadline, if he didn't do what was expected of him.

He might be a fool about plenty, but not when it came to Mother. He'd agreed to come for Christmas and to stay . . . indefinitely.

Blast it all.

"Still. I don't know why a little thing like not knowing I existed should have stopped you from giving me advice." Cyril flashed a smile, though he kept his gaze out the window. The village of Castleton trotted by, every doorway wreathed or swagged with greenery, every window bedecked with holly and ivy and mistletoe, every lamppost adorned with a red bow.

It really did look like a scene from a Christmas card.

"My apologies, sir. I'll do better in any future past we stumble across."

"See that you do." He spotted the church steeple in the village's central square, but the carriage turned rather than driving directly past it. He tried to recall if Lord Castleton had taken his family to the midnight service on Christmas Eve . . . he didn't think so. Wasn't their big ball on Christmas Eve? He'd have to check the calendar that Kellie had begun for him. But if not at midnight, the whole family would no doubt go on Christmas morning. Something to look forward to, at least.

"Are you ready to tell me about this branch of the family yet?" Kellie's voice sounded challenging, but Cyril knew well it was more probing. Inviting.

Because every other time over the last sixteen months his valet had tried to bring them up, Cyril had said he didn't want to talk about them. Which he didn't. But it seemed that leisure was expired, so he sighed and watched the village's businesses give way to homes. Smaller buildings, but no less festooned.

21

"Lord Castleton is my fifth cousin." It was as good a place as any to begin. "He apparently remained a bachelor longer than most, though the reason was never told to me. When finally he married, it was to a widow of a viscount who already had three children. Louise is the eldest. Fred is the middle child, four years younger than her and within a few months of me, actually."

Kellie lifted his brows. "A built-in friend when you last came?"

"You'd think so, but no." He directed his frown back out the window. "He'd just started at Eton, and according to the youngest sibling, Mariah, it had made him insufferable." His lips tugged up of their own will, still able to see her standing in the family's sitting room, a doll in her arms and anger sparking in her eyes. "I can't say if he was any better before school. But I can attest to his insufferableness then."

"And Lady Mariah is the youngest, then?"

Cyril nodded. "She was the one I befriended. Louise was . . . well, already on the cusp of adulthood at fifteen and having no patience for childish things. Fred was an absolute bore. So Mariah and I spent most of the holiday outside, exploring and playing."

"That doesn't sound so bad."

"It wasn't." An understatement, actually. He'd had a shockingly marvelous holiday at Mariah's side, creating whole worlds together. But then he'd overheard that sentiment of Castleton's before he left, and it had soured his whole memory. Even so, for years he and Mariah had exchanged letters once a week—he'd have called her not just a friend, but one of his *best* friends, despite the fact that he never returned to Plumford.

But time wrought its sad way, as it too often did. Round about the time that she was fifteen and he was heading to university, the letters had begun to shift in tone. They'd both put away childish things, that was all. Grown into themselves. And it seemed that the selves they'd grown into no longer had anything in common. The letters had first shifted and then tapered off and finally stopped altogether.

Another reason he dreaded this visit. A reason, frankly, he'd avoided London as long as the Castletons were there. He didn't know exactly who this new, grown-up Mariah was . . . only that she wasn't the Mariah he knew. The one he'd *wanted* to see again.

"So Lord and Lady Castleton never had children of their own?"

At that, Cyril winced. "They did. A son. But he was stillborn, and the birth was so traumatic and . . . damaging to the lady that, ah . . . quite impossible, they said, for her to have another child. And given that it's been fourteen years since then, no one sees any reason to doubt the physicians." He certainly wasn't going to. There were things a gentleman simply didn't ask.

He could practically see Kellie doing the maths in his head. "So then it was a few years after that when he called upon you?"

"He had to hire a historian to trace the lineage back and then an investigator to track us down." Cyril probably shouldn't take pride in how difficult it had been, but for whatever reason, it had been satisfying to realize how much effort it had taken. Childish of him, no doubt. But then, he'd been a child when he learned of it.

And at the time, the thought of being so far away from his father's family had been thrilling indeed. At this point, the memories were distant, but they hadn't been then. Father had been a hard man. Cruel, when the mood struck. And it had begun striking more and more often before the sickness that hit him hard and fast had stolen his life.

Cyril had known that a good boy would have mourned him. He'd been too relieved to know how—and bordering on giddy when his mother had packed him up and left the Lightbourne home, returning to her own family seat in Hampshire. "That first visit was just an introduction. To verify I wasn't a dunce and was fit to be trained up, I suppose. But Mother insisted I be raised among her family, and he relented. He paid for my schooling, though."

"Something to thank him for."

"I have done." Every Christmas, and on the earl's birthday too, he sent a long, compliant letter full of his accomplishments and gratitude that his lordship had made them possible—and he'd meant every word, given how much he loved the world of academia. Castleton inevitably replied with his pleasure and pride.

But it was a distant, unfamiliar pleasure. An empty, hollow pride. They were strangers still. And that scared ten-year-old still hovering within him was none too sure that any amount of time spent at Plumford Hall would change that. What if Castleton was just like Cyril's father? What if Mariah had been so eager to play outside in order to escape him? She'd never breathed a word of that and always seemed fond of him . . . but children of monsters learned quickly to keep their fear buttoned up tight. He knew that all too well.

The carriage slowed, the driver's "Whoa! Whoa there!" loud enough to draw both him and Kellie to the windows and to open them wide so they could see what brought them to a rocking, clanging halt. Cyril poked his head out, and his eyes went wide. A cart full of evergreen boughs and what looked like four large trees had overturned. He jumped out half a second before he heard Kellie do the same from the opposite side.

Though snow frosted the grass and trees, the road was relatively clear. His boots had no trouble finding traction as he jogged toward the accident.

A man garbed in stout winter clothing stood with a hand on the bridle of the enormous draft horse currently unhitched, another man standing beside the overturned wagon.

"Is anyone hurt?" Cyril shouted as he drew near, searching the ground for any other limbs of person instead of tree.

The two looked up and over as if just noticing the arrival of a carriage—and gaped when they spotted it. Not, Cyril knew, because of who it carried. But because of the crest on its side.

Castleton had sent it to pick him up from the train station in the neighboring village of Hope.

"We're both fine, sir," the one by the wagon said, doffing his cap. "Just fine. Thank you kindly for asking."

Fear? No, it didn't seem like it. It was more curiosity that colored his tone. Cyril smiled. "What happened?" He expected a wheel to have come off the axle, but that didn't appear to be the case.

The man sent a scowl toward his partner. Or, no. Toward the horse. "That ornery Scabbard, that's what happened. Decided to jump into the ditch for no apparent reason, then out again, and it tipped the wagon."

The horse shook its head and snorted, seemingly put out at the insult to his behavior.

Kellie had come up alongside Cyril. "Well, perhaps we can help you right it."

"Oh, we couldn't ask that of a couple of gents like you," the man said, waving a hand as if to dismiss them. "My brother'll be coming along soon enough with a second load. He can help us, and we'll get these Christmas trees up to the manor house in no time."

"We're not a couple of gents," Kellie said, grinning, his Irish coming out. "Just one, and he's a sorry excuse for one, at that. Plenty educated, but not really trained up yet, you know."

"I beg your pardon." Cyril let his Oxford intonations shine through, but then smiled. "Happy to lend a hand, though." He strode toward the locals. "Mr. Cyril Lightbourne, and this is Aiden Kellie."

He knew saying his surname in these parts would come with some recognition, but he was surprised at the quick flash of pleasure across both men's faces. The first fellow took his proffered hand with far more enthusiasm than he deserved.

"His lordship's heir! A true honor to meet you, sir. A true honor. We're most excited for the chance to get to know you in the coming months and years, ain't we, Joe?"

Joe let go of Scabbard's bridle and was coming forward with his hand out, too, his face just as bright. "Indeed, indeed we are! Happy Christmas to you, sir. And won't our wives be jealous when they hear we've met you already and haven't had to wait for the ball!"

Kellie darted Cyril a questioning look, but apparently his face was blank enough that his valet thought he'd better ask the obvious question aloud. "Forgive me—I dunno much about this ball yet. It's for . . . ?"

"Oh, the whole neighborhood. Rich and poor alike, it is. Highlight of our year. The kiddiewinks can never wait to see what treats Lady Mariah and Mrs. Trutchen have made for them this time, and what toy the good professor has crafted for them."

Professor? Cyril had no memory of a professor in residence . . . though the thought of Lady Mariah devising treats for the village children made something long unsettled shift a few degrees toward peace inside him.

Maybe she hadn't changed quite as much as he feared. Maybe revisiting Plumford wouldn't be all cold feelings. Even if Lady Pearl's parting, sneering prediction still set his teeth on edge. *"Go to your long-lost cousin's estate, where it won't matter that you're a sorry excuse for a gentleman. I'm certain one of his stepdaughters will be tossed at you anyway, to keep the property in the family."*

He wasn't interested in having Mariah or Louise—she was widowed now, wasn't she?—tossed at him. But he was supremely interested in a friend, either in one of the daughters or in Fred. They were adults now, on more equal footing. The hope of real relationships with the family wasn't altogether impossible, was it?

He offered a smile to the men and moved with Kellie and the one who wasn't Joe to the grounded side of the wagon. "Well, friends, I for one can't wait to see what treats lie in store for us either. So let's get you righted, shall we?"

Not-Joe grinned, and Joe gripped the skyward side of the wagon. "On three, then. One . . . two . . . three."

The wagon crashed back onto its wheels, sending a shower of pine needles over them like fragrant green snowfall. Cyril couldn't help but laugh.

No, maybe this wouldn't be so horrible a Christmas after all.

Mariah found Papa exactly where she'd expected him to
be—in the small library attached to his study, sitting in
his favorite leather chair, which he'd angled toward the window
rather than the fireplace. He was brooding in a way better suited
to young Joy's little brother than to a man of distinguished years,
and it made her grin as she padded softly into the room.

She sat on the arm of his chair and draped her own arm around
his shoulders. Her gaze followed his to the drive, only visible from
here because of the bare limbs of the trees. Empty still, though
Cyril was due any moment. "I do hope you're getting the sulk out
of your system now, Papa. If you greet him like this, he'll tuck tail
and run, and then where would we be?"

Rather than chuckle, Papa sighed and patted her hand. "I have
no argument with the young man himself. He got good marks in
school, is reportedly of excellent character. But that's the very
thing—I only know him from reports. His line is so far removed
from the family tree that he's scarcely related at all. It isn't right
that everything should go to him."

Mariah leaned over to rest her cheek on the top of his head.
She knew how deeply her stepfather loved Plumford Manor and
all of Castleton. She knew it because she'd seen it every day of her

memory, because she'd been always at his knee as a child, learning to love it too. The house and the land and, most of all, the people. Papa had always been the best sort of landlord, who tried to give his neighbors dreams and the wings to chase them, not to lash them to this one place for his own benefit. He sponsored countless children who wanted to go on to higher learning, looked for innovative ways to improve life for everyone, and he always put their well-being above his own profit.

She wasn't certain anymore whether his love for this place had inspired her own because of how much she loved him . . . or if perhaps she was so close to him because of their shared love for Plumford and the neighborhood. Or if it was some combination thereof.

Regardless, she could sigh along with him because she understood his desire to hold fast to what he'd worked so hard for. And she could pray, as she'd done so many times over the last quiet years, that Cyril Lightbourne would come to love it just as deeply.

"Everything will work out, Papa." She used her most soothing voice, even though it hadn't the melody of Louise's or the richness of Mama's. "You'll see. Now that Cyril is coming for good, it will only be a matter of time until he feels like a son to you."

Papa let out another laborious sigh. "So you say, sweetling. But sometimes I think there must be some flaw in my character that keeps me from forming such bonds. I have tried my best to be a father to all you children, but you're the only one . . ."

She gave him a squeeze, kissed the top of his head again. "Through no fault, Papa. No fault at all. It's only that Louise was already eleven when you and Mama married, and she missed our father so. And Fred has always felt that pull back to that other home he always knew was his. But they both love you. They love how you love Mama. They respect and honor you."

His hum at once granted and dismissed her point, while his eyes kept their watch on the empty drive. "I wish . . . I wish the choice were mine. On who inherits, I mean."

She chuckled at the very thought, because she knew well what he meant. He knew that she loved this place as he did, and that she was the only one—thus far, at least—who did so. He'd said before that he wished he could leave it in her care. But law after law prohibited that.

"Well," she began, "we should petition the king. Not only to break the entail on the property, but to allow for a woman to inherit the title. And to specify that the woman needn't even be a blood relative. That you ought to be able to appoint an heir of your choosing. I can't imagine the king would mind."

He snorted a laugh at the joke and squeezed her hand again. He and the king were friends, but even friendship couldn't work such miracles. "If only, sweetling. If only. As it is . . ." He turned his head a bit, and she took that glimmer in his eyes as warning.

Enough of one that she sat up straight on the arm of the chair, shaking her head. "Don't. Don't even say it."

"It's the traditional answer. Expected, even."

"I'm not going to marry Cyril just because it's convenient!" Papa, of all people, ought to understand that. Hadn't he remained a bachelor for so many years because he couldn't stand the thought of sharing his life with a woman he didn't love wholeheartedly? But then he'd met Mama, just coming out of mourning for Mariah's father. How could he begrudge Mariah a marriage built on the same warm foundation?

Her heart burned within her, enough that she knew the flames would show in her eyes. She averted them, taking up the vigil of the window. Mama and Papa had both been hinting for years that she ought to try to win Cyril's favor. And it always tied her up in knots. Because she had won his favor, when they were children and she hadn't known she should. In the two weeks they'd spent together over that Christmas holiday when she was seven and he was ten, she'd written him as the prince in her fairy-tale endings.

And for years afterward, their letters had kept them close. But then, when she turned fifteen, Mama had insisted upon overseeing

Mariah's correspondence with him, and she'd made her edit out the "silliness," saying she must present herself as a proper young lady, one worthy of becoming the next Lady Castleton, mistress of Plumford Manor.

Was that why he'd stopped writing back? Or had it just been that the tides of life had separated them too much? Regardless, they were strangers again now, as proven by the fact that he'd cast his heart at the feet of Lady Pearl.

The flames twisted within her, stinging tears to her eyes that she blinked away. For too many years, she'd hoped Cyril Lightbourne would return—not just to Plumford, but to her. She'd dreamed of him. Placed so many hopes on him. But year after year, season after season, he'd stayed away. And then her first word of him in ages was *that*. If she'd retained any hope of that oh-so-convenient match, the mention of Lady Pearl had dashed it. And if her parents all but shoved *her* at him, he'd already proven himself the type to care only for passing things, so how could she even consider him? An old friend who saw her only as a convenience was even worse, somehow, than a stranger who looked right through her.

Papa took her hand in his again. "You know I want only the best for you, Mariah. Whether that means Plumford or some other place. Perhaps even . . . some other kingdom?"

She sighed and tried to tug her fingers free. Speaking of strangers who looked right through her . . . "If you're thinking of the Dane, banish the thought. He didn't even like me."

"Why then would he have requested this visit? And why would he have made specific mention of you?"

She knew very well his reasons—and they were her brother and stepfather and their family's association with the Crown. The greve had made no secret of only looking among England's most noteworthy families for his bride. "Not for affection, I promise you that."

Papa chuckled. "Only because he hasn't spent enough time with you to be charmed. But he will be, I have no doubt. You'll have your pick of two fine gentlemen by the end of the holiday, I daresay."

Hardly. What she would have was a week or two spent in the company of not one but *two* gentlemen who just wanted to sing Lady Pearl's praises. Utter torture. "We'll see, I suppose."

"Mm." Papa's narrowed eyes said he saw right through her docile words. "Please don't dismiss him, Mariah. He's an intimate of the Danish king—not a man to be trifled with, or of whom one should make an enemy. More, he's showing us a great honor by spending the holiday with us. I may selfishly wish you'd choose Cyril instead, but this could be an unparalleled match."

She stood from her perch and stalked over to the window, hoping Papa wouldn't see how her fingers dug into the arms she'd crossed. He said it like she would have an actual choice to make, like either of those men would want *her*. As if the fact that they both preferred Pearl didn't speak so very eloquently about them.

Mariah and Pearl had been together at finishing school, and Pearl was . . . *monstrous* was the only word Mariah could think of. A spoiled brat of a girl, so enamored with her own beauty and position that she thought the rest of the world ought to bow to her and do her bidding.

And the idiot men of London had certainly agreed. She'd debuted to huge success last Season, and it wasn't jealousy that set Mariah's teeth on edge. It was that she knew Pearl's true colors, knew very well she'd gone into the Season planning to string along as many men as possible before choosing the best match. Knew that she kept many of those beaux on her string to spite the other young ladies rather than from any genuine interest.

She puffed her breath out through her nose and failed at fighting off a wave of despair.

Papa came up beside her, no doubt more words about the virtues of Lord Gyldenkrone ready on his tongue, but Cyril unwittingly rescued her from the impending lecture as his carriage rolled up the drive. Her heart squeezed at the sight, and she didn't know if it was dread or some dormant hope struggling to life. "There he is."

Papa drew in a long, fortifying breath and squared his shoulders. "Quite right. Well, then. Shall we welcome him properly home?"

Mariah tucked her hand into Papa's elbow and hurried with him down the stairs to the front entrance of the house. Had the weather been milder, they would have gathered the whole family and upper staff outside to welcome him properly, but given the bitter cold, no one—Cyril included—would appreciate that. So instead, the plan was to stage the welcome in the main hall, just inside the doors, with the impressive staircases curving up behind them on either side.

She knew well that a footman had been assigned the task of lookout, and the alert rang through the halls as they walked—bells and shouts ringing. She couldn't help but think it sounded appropriate to the season in general, which brought a smile back to her lips.

They were still awaiting the last loads of greenery, but even without it, the house looked beautiful, decked out in its Christmas finery. Her heart thrilled a little more with each decoration they passed and each smile she caught on the faces of the maids still at work.

Mama and Louise were hurrying down the opposite staircase as Mariah and Papa descended theirs. Fred had likely been in the billiards room, given that he was emerging from the west corridor, looking annoyed by the interruption. On the one hand, she couldn't blame him—Cyril wasn't the heir to his home, after all, and Fred had been so busy learning the Lyons estate in recent years that he'd been rather desperate for this holiday with his family. He'd not been happy to learn that they'd have other guests too. On the other hand, if her brother didn't choose to smile now and then, those frown lines would take him over altogether. He was well on his way to becoming a veritable Scrooge.

Mariah took her place in the line of family—Papa, Mama, Louise, Fred, and then finally her at the far left—and cast a smile over her shoulder at the row of staff. The housekeeper and butler, Mr. and Mrs. Dunover, Mrs. Trutchen, the three ladies' maids and two valets, and the row of polished footmen. They each returned her smile, the cook tossing in a dimpled wink and holding out a little bag toward her.

After making certain her parents were paying her no heed, she reached back for the ribbon-tied sack, able to tell from its shape what it contained. Mrs. Trutchen always brought Mariah the first finished sugar plums if Mariah wasn't in the kitchen when they came out of the oven. The sugar plums were still a bit warm, and her mouth watered at the very thought of them. She held the bag up to inhale deeply of the fragrance wafting from it and smiled anew. The smell was surely reminiscent of heaven itself.

But she didn't untie it and select one to eat here and now, much as she wanted to. She could only imagine the frown Mama would send her way if she greeted Papa's heir with a mouthful of sticky confection.

She could hear the creak and jingle of the carriage drawing near and then halting. The doorman watched the progress of their guest from his chair at the side window, and he sprang into action as Cyril neared, throwing both doors wide in a gesture of welcome reserved only for the most important guests.

And better suited to summer. Icy wind blew into the hall, making them all shiver and earning surprised gasps from the ladies too. A few snow flurries danced their way inside, creating a whirl in the center of which came Cyril Lightbourne, who had bounded up the marble steps in order to enter more quickly.

As the doors were closed again behind him, Cyril came to a halt in the center of their little half circle. His attention went exactly where it should—to Papa. Which left Mariah free to catalogue his every changed feature.

He was taller. As tall as Fred, putting him at least a half foot above Mariah. He wore a dark grey suit that fit him well but was clearly not as expensive as either Papa's or Fred's. It was covered with an inverness cape coat, which she'd always thought rather dashing, if for no other reason than it made quite a flair when one took it off, as Cyril did now, along with his hat, when the doorman stepped forward to receive them.

But what made that long-cinched knot of dread loosen inside her was his face. He looked like Cyril. The boy she remembered, just a bit more chiseled, the round cheeks of youth slimmed down. Handsome not only because of his features but because of the light in his eyes, the genuineness of his smile.

Not the sort of Adonis that Pearl favored, honestly. Not normally. Did that mean that the attraction was something more genuine? That love had made the shallow beauty see something deeper? Had Cyril somehow drawn depth from Pearl that Mariah had never seen?

Papa stepped forward, and perhaps he saw the same goodness in Cyril's eyes, because his own smile of greeting didn't look forced. He shook Cyril's hand with his right, clapped his left to the younger man's shoulder. "Welcome . . . welcome."

Welcome home was what he'd planned to say, and the missing word made Mariah's brow crease for a moment. Apparently Papa still needed a bit of warming-up time. But Cyril must not have heard the lack. He shook her papa's hand, nodded, and neither his smile nor his eyes dimmed. "Thank you, my lord. I'm . . . glad to be here."

She suspected something was missing or edited in his words too. Before she could guess at what it was, he'd turned to Mama. "Lady Castleton, you've grown more lovely since I saw you last."

Mama chuckled, dismissive even though it was true, and took his hands in hers. She then leaned over and up to kiss his cheek. "Welcome back to Plumford Manor, Cyril. We're so glad you've come."

Louise greeted him next, with a hand extended for its obligatory kiss, murmuring the expected words with the expected smile and very little feeling. Fred shook his hand with a rather short "How do you do?" that was answered and returned. Those two, it seemed, were no more inclined to be friends now than they'd been as children.

And then he was in front of her, and Mariah couldn't for the life of her remember what Mama had instructed her to say. She could only think, *Yes. This is Cyril.* The boy who had helped turn the plum orchards, the little lake, the wood into a fairyland with her. The boy who had laughed and dreamed with her. He was still there, shining in the eyes of this man. A friend, waiting to become reacquainted.

She held out the bag of confections and let her relief spill into her smile. "Welcome to Sugar Plum Manor, Cyril."

Would he remember the name they'd given the estate in their play? The quick flash of his smile said he did, and he laughed in delight as he opened the bag and drew out one of the freshly baked treats. They'd been his favorite, too, and he inhaled their scent with pure bliss on his face. "You remembered." He sounded amazed by the fact.

As if forgetting had been possible. "I still have the story we wrote together." That hadn't been part of her script either, but so long as she didn't glance over at Mama, she couldn't be chided for it. "I actually helped the village children turn it into a Christmas play. You've missed the performance by a few days, but they did a marvelous job with it."

"Oh for heaven's sake." Fred turned to them, his scowl deeper than ever. "He doesn't care about some stupid story you wrote when you were seven, Ri, nor about the ridiculous school play the children put on. Just leave the man alone, will you?"

Once upon a time, Fred had indulged her fancies, played her games with her. But she found those times harder and harder to remember when he behaved like this. Yet the change, the harsh tones, never failed to sting. Much like it had stung when he'd not only failed to come on a train early enough to see that "ridiculous

36

play" she'd worked so hard on, but had arrived *during* the performance, so that her parents missed it too as they went to fetch him.

Cyril's eyes flashed with temper, and his chin lifted a notch. "On
the contrary, Lord Lyons. I can think of nothing more entertaining
than revisiting the story your sister and I composed together." He
flashed a grin. "I daresay it holds up quite well against the literature
I've been studying, geniuses that we were."

Ah yes. Still Cyril. The only one even close to her age who had
ever defended her to Fred or Louise. At age seven, she would have
punctuated Cyril's defense by sticking out her tongue at Fred. A
sore temptation even now, but she refrained—and accepted the
sugar plum Cyril handed her before he took another for himself
and took a bite.

She did too, her heart pattering happily as the taste exploded
on her well-behaved tongue and her brother rolled his eyes and
turned away.

Papa and Mama had both turned toward them, Mama's eyes
spitting warnings and reprimands at Fred and Papa looking from
Cyril to Mariah with so many thoughts playing across his face
that she couldn't keep up.

He smiled, though, and held out an arm toward the drawing
room. "Won't you join us for some more substantial refreshments
while your things are unpacked? We would love to hear the updates
that never fit in a letter before Gyldenkrone arrives tomorrow."

Cyril had been turning to follow Papa's indicative arm, but at
the greve's name, he froze, something that looked strangely like
apprehension in his eyes. "Gyldenkrone, did you say? Which one,
if I may ask?"

Papa's brows rose. "The elder brother—the greve. You are familiar with him?"

"Somewhat, yes. More so with his brother, Emil." His eye
twitched as he said it, and Mariah frowned. Was that a bruise
faintly lining the skin beneath his eye? Or perhaps merely shadows
of exhaustion from his travels?

"Ah. Well, I have no doubt the two of you will get on famously. But we shall cherish the day with only you before he arrives—and then, after the holidays, we shall settle into a true routine." He paused, his face going earnest. "We want Plumford to be your home, Cyril. Your true home."

There. Mariah smiled, proud of him for saying it—and for meaning it.

Cyril measured him for a long moment, as if gauging his sincerity. Then, at last, he nodded. "That is my hope too."

4

$\mathcal{S}$omehow Cyril had forgotten that Plumford Manor—or Sugar Plum Manor, as he and Mariah had dubbed it twelve years ago as they feasted on their favorite candy—was even more charming than the Christmas-card–worthy village of Castleton. Over the years, those overheard words of the earl echoing always in his heart, he'd told himself it was a dreary, drafty place. Dark and brooding. Foreboding. Unwelcoming. Like a haunted house in one of the Gothic novels he'd read too many of as an adolescent.

That story had been a lie, and he realized it the moment he stepped inside. It wasn't the twinkling electric lights—his own mother's home didn't have those yet—or the festive decorations everywhere he looked. It was the brilliant smiles on the faces of the staff, the genuine excitement in their eyes at his arrival, the care with which each piece of furniture in each room was tended.

He'd visited a few other manor houses over the years, as he holidayed with school chums or toured points of interest. He knew it was, in fact, easy for them to be nothing but shells of their former glory, or to feel more dungeon than castle.

Not Plumford, though. Its every crackling hearth and cinnamon-scented room sang out that this house, for all its imposing beauty, was a home. And as the lord and lady led the way into the drawing room, he remembered quite suddenly how on the day they'd first welcomed him, he'd been struck by longing for it to be *his* home.

It struck him again now, despite himself. Not a coveting of the things—just a desire to belong. Something that he'd never quite found anywhere else.

He turned to the Lyons siblings, knowing he ought to offer his arm to Louise, as the elder lady, but wishing he could pretend he didn't know that. If one were only to compare their features, she was the more beautiful of the sisters—but her eyes were cool and distant, her rigid posture shouting that she wanted to escape the company as quickly as she could. He would have preferred to walk in with Mariah.

He'd missed her. He hadn't realized it, not really. It had been too easy to convince himself that the person he'd missed wasn't there anymore, that she'd grown into . . . well, into Louise. But the young woman who'd greeted him hadn't been cool and composed. She'd been *Mariah*, the one he'd counted as such a good friend for so long. He didn't know why the tone of her letters had changed in the last four years, but clearly some of the old Mariah still lurked inside her, if only trotted out for Christmas.

He bit back a sigh and offered his arm to Louise, who rested her hand on his forearm so lightly that it hovered more than it touched. That made him have to bite back a grin along with the sigh. She couldn't have made her opinion of him any clearer had she actually deigned to speak instead of keeping her face directed toward her mother's back.

Fred, he noted, didn't escort his younger sister in. He merely strode ahead, found a chair, and slouched into it. No, he didn't slouch. His posture remained perfect. Yet he somehow put off the air of his discontent without his shoulders following his attitude's lead. Remarkable, really. Cyril would have to study him a bit to sort out how he managed it.

Louise reclaimed her hand and moved to the settee closest to the fire, giving him a polite imitation of a smile as she abandoned him. Mariah slipped in behind them and took the same chair she'd favored as a child. He moved to the one beside hers—the one he'd claimed as his own before—with the polished mahogany end table between them.

As he sat and the countess rang for tea, he let their impending guest's name strike him again. *Gyldenkrone*. Not Emil—but even so. Was it coincidence that one of the Danish brothers was coming here? That band of pressure around his chest warned him that it wasn't, though it seemed a bit self-centered to think that the greve would be following him to Castleton. Why should he? His fight had been with Emil, not Søren.

They were a tight-knit pair. Different as night and day, but family honor and reputation was the byword of them both. Maybe Søren was looking for satisfaction?

Blast. He hoped not. The last thing he wanted was to bring any unpleasantness here for Christmas. So as casually as he could, he smiled and asked, "So Lord Gyldenkrone—I wasn't aware that he was a friend of yours?"

Castleton chuckled and glanced at Mariah. "Not exactly. We were introduced in London last summer. I offered to show him about the Peak District anytime he wanted to visit. He just accepted the offer—no doubt wanting to escape London for the holiday. And wanting, too, he said, the chance to get to know our Mariah better."

That band around his chest went even tighter. Mariah and Gyldenkrone? He knew that sometimes opposites attracted, but *Gyldenkrone*? He'd just stood by while his brother insulted the last lady he claimed to be courting. What sort of man did that?

Not one with any nobility in his spirit, that was certain. Not one with a bit of warmth in his heart. Gyldenkrone might be a favorite of the Danish king, but he was little better than a villain to Cyril's way of thinking. He'd had the perfect opportunity to prove himself a hero and had just stood by, letting Emil defame Lady Pearl.

That sort of chap didn't deserve a young lady as sweet as Cyril's old friend.

Realizing that the earl still awaited some reply from him, Cyril smiled. "Well, I certainly can't blame him for that. I'm rather looking forward to getting to know her again myself." Turning back to Mariah, he let his smile turn to a grin. "Tell me, my lady—how is our nutcracker doing?"

When he'd come last time, his mother had sent him with small gifts for each member of the family, though the ones for the children hadn't been assigned per se, as much as given to him as a collection to be dispensed at will. He'd assumed that Fred would be the one who'd appreciate the military uniform of the wooden nutcracker figure, but he'd sneered at it and opted for the box of toffee. Louise had claimed the doll Mother had made with the younger sister in mind, leaving Mariah with the nutcracker.

She'd claimed to love it, called it the most handsome thing she'd ever seen, and had carried it about with her on their adventures. And up until that shift four years ago, she'd even added a postscript to her every letter of "Nutcracker sends his greetings."

Fred snorted. He, of course, had made endless fun of her for her preference. "It's still sitting on her mantel year-round—the ugly thing."

Sentimental of her—and unexpected. He'd have thought she'd rid her room of her childhood things by now, much as she'd rid her correspondence of them.

The tea cart was wheeled in, and conversation turned toward whether he still favored this or that confection, how he now took his tea, and didn't he just love this pattern of Wedgwood? It was one of the first sets the famed potter had fired and was how Queen Charlotte had been introduced to him, though that story was never told outside their own house. . . .

The talk was pleasant, amiable—aside from a few comments from Fred that Cyril had no difficulty in ignoring. He had to admit that the unwelcome he feared seeing in Lord Castleton's eyes was but a dim, unwilling flicker, if there at all. Maybe Kellie was right. Maybe their problems could be resolved simply by becoming familiar.

Eventually, the ladies excused themselves—or rather, Lady Castleton did and insisted her daughters join her. Fred declared himself bound for the billiards room again and invited Cyril to join him at some point "when he was ready for normal male entertainments," and he was left alone with the earl.

Cyril's every muscle went taut, but after a long moment of unabashed studying of him, Castleton smiled. Not the bright, welcoming smile of a host for a guest. A small, genuine smile that he surely didn't bandy about so freely. "Cyril," he said slowly.

Cyril slid his now-empty plate onto the side table. "My lord?"

The earl tapped a finger against the arm of the settee. "May I ask you a question?"

The cake he'd eaten settled like a stone. "Of course you may."

"Why have you not returned until now?"

He should have expected the question. *Had* expected it. And yet had let himself hope that they could sweep the last twelve years under the rug and ignore them. Suddenly wishing there was more tea in his cup, he cleared his throat. "May I be frank, my lord?"

If they were going to do this—make themselves family, make this Cyril's true home—then he couldn't let that old bitterness fester any longer. He had to come clean.

Castleton nodded, interest sparking in his blue eyes.

Cyril sighed. "My last day here, before I was scheduled to leave, I went to find you. To thank you for your hospitality and assure you I would do all in my power to make you proud. Only, when I approached your study, you were there with your wife, and . . . well, I eavesdropped."

Rather than chide him for the old sin, the earl went still, then sighed. "I don't recall the conversation. But I can guess at it."

Cyril nodded, but it turned into a sagging of his chin to his chest. "You said something about how you couldn't bear your

43

legacy going to a stranger. I took that to mean that you couldn't bear the thought of me at all—that you resented my very existence."

"Resented it?" Castleton straightened. "If it weren't for your existence, my title would go extinct when I die, and if I couldn't break the entail, everything I have would revert to the Crown. You couldn't think I'd want that."

Cyril dared a glance up. "Put like that, of course not. And yet I knew I wasn't your choice."

The earl raked a hand through his steel-grey hair. "I must beg your forgiveness, Cyril. You're right. I searched for my heir because I had to, but I resented needing to turn to a stranger. Even so, I never meant for you to hear such a sentiment. I wanted to bring you into our family then. To get to know you. To . . . to make you my son." His gaze darted to the doorway. "Something Fred certainly never wanted to be. In his eyes, I never compared to his father."

Cyril's throat went tight. He forced a smile to his lips, though it felt crooked. "Well, my lord, I can assure you that you outshine mine—even with my misinterpretation of your opinion of me."

Castleton's eyes clouded over with a frown. "The investigator's report included a bit of your father's . . . history. Some of your old neighbors had brought some not-so-small charges against him before he died."

"Which you quieted." Or so Mother had told him, eventually.

It must have sounded as much like an accusation to the earl's ears as it did to his own. "Not for his sake, my boy. For yours. That kind of stain follows a family for generations. Had he been alive still, then perhaps there would have been value in justice. But he was already gone, so why should you be haunted forever by being identified as the son of a criminal?"

Because he hadn't just been a thief or a forger. He'd hurt people. And as one of them who'd borne his bruises, Cyril had hoped he'd be condemned for it, even if posthumously.

He could see the earl's point, though. Now. "I suppose you're right."

"I don't know if I was or not. I know your mother accused me of paying off the witnesses, but it wasn't that—not to my eyes, at least. I compensated the victims as best I could. I paid for their medical expenses and restored the property he'd destroyed. It was the most I could do to try to rectify the damage he'd done." His cheeks flushed. "I admit I was embarrassed that anyone bearing the name of Lightbourne should have behaved so abominably. That is not what our family stands for."

Remembering the joviality and health of everyone he'd seen in the village, Cyril nodded. "I owe you an apology, too, it seems, my lord. I didn't understand any of your actions when I was a child. But I clung to my childish thoughts instead of seeking the truth as I grew up. That was wrong of me. I let my own fears and insecurities keep me from returning to Plumford. I see now . . ." He had to pause, swallow. "I see now that I've missed the chance to forge a relationship with you and your family. And I'm sorry for that."

"Well." The earl blinked a few rapid times and gave him another earnest little smile. "Happily, the future lies before us, and we needn't let those past mistakes shackle us. We can start anew, eh? Today."

Shackle was the right word—because he felt them fall, felt his spirit rise as free as Paul set loose by the Spirit. "Yes. I would like nothing more."

"Excellent." Slapping his hands to his knees, the earl stood. "I won't take more of your time now. I know after a day's travel you'll be eager to tidy up or even stretch your legs and get some exercise. But I want you to know that from this day onward, I want you to view Plumford Manor as your own. Your home. Catalogue any changes you would want to make, poke into any crevice, ask any question you have. And—" A knowing gleam entered the earl's eyes. "Feel free to invite any guests you desire. I hear there's a certain young lady who may be interested in a tour of your inheritance? Eh?"

Cyril felt his neck go hot. "I beg your pardon?"

Obviously interpreting his flush as embarrassment over his affections being known rather than over them being squashed by a lady who would most assuredly *not* be coming for a visit, the earl chuckled. "No need to play the innocent, my boy. The gossip columns have been abuzz with whether or not the newcomer, Mr. L, heir to Lord C, will soon be engaged to Lady P, daughter of Lord K. It's no secret who any of those letters are, you know." Walking with him from the drawing room, Castleton gave him a friendly elbow to the ribs. "Quite the coup, I hear. Lady Pearl was the belle of the Season."

Cyril had deliberately arrived in London *after* the Season, but he'd heard the tales of the dozens of young aristocrats vying for her hand. "So I learned."

"I know my wife is dying for the story of how the two of you met. Something about a rescue, wasn't it?"

Cyril cleared his throat. "She was in a little boat with her friends, and somehow they managed to overturn it. The other young ladies swam to shore, but she can't swim. I was walking by and saw her struggling and dove in."

"Her hero." The sparkle in the earl's eyes made Cyril wonder if it was really the countess who had wanted the story. "Fit for a fairy tale, that meeting."

He'd thought so. And he'd certainly been dazzled by her beauty and her gratitude. As he became acquainted with her reputation, he'd hoped that perhaps that vulnerable moment they'd shared had, in fact, given them a bond she'd not forged with any other. That she'd shown him the authentic part of herself she kept hidden from her other scores of admirers. He'd thought this was his story, the one in which he'd get to be someone worthy, the one in which he'd discover why the Lord had made him as He had, that it would be the first step toward a life worth living. Worth, someday, writing about.

More the fool, him.

He ought to correct the earl here and now. Tell him that Pearl had ended things. But that gloomy end hadn't yet made the public rounds, and he was loath to invite it into his Christmas. So he offered a muted version of the truth. "Lady Pearl and I are nowhere near a betrothal, I promise you. She is, in fact, notoriously fickle with her attention. I would be surprised if she even remembers me come the new year."

"Oh now, give yourself some credit!"

The sentiment—or rather, that the earl actually seemed to feel it—cheered him. Cyril smiled. "Regardless. For now, I'm quite content to concentrate on this family. You can't know how much it means to me."

The sparkle in Castleton's eyes didn't dim. He reached over and gripped Cyril's shoulder. "I think you mean that *only* I could know how much it means to you. For it means just the same to me. Perhaps more."

They'd exited the room and stood now in the great hall again.

"I'll show you to your suite. Gyldenkrone will be in the bachelor wing, but as you are family and not a guest, you'll have rooms in the main house with us. If that suits you?"

It was where he'd stayed as a child, but he hadn't dared expect the same welcome now. "Of course, my lord."

"Oh, enough of that. Call me Castleton—or Cass, as my friends do. Or some more familial diminutive? I realize I'm not actually an uncle, and so distant a cousin that even that sounds odd, but I wouldn't mind either moniker."

Cyril smiled. "I'll think on it. Try a few out, perhaps. We'll see what suits us both." And wouldn't Kellie rib him eternally when he heard how quickly Cyril's fears had been dispelled? A ribbing he was happily saved from when Castleton hadn't done more than point to his door on the upper floor before another opened at the opposite end of the hallway and Mariah stepped out, papers clutched in her hand.

He paused, glancing inside his open door but scarcely registering the pleasant blues and greens. Far more interesting was the shy, hesitant excitement in her step. He moved away from his room rather than into it. "Is that the story?"

Mariah held it up with a grin. "The very same. I have no doubt that our handwriting will horrify you, as it did me when I dug this out last month to turn it into a script for the children."

He chuckled and glanced at her stepfather. "Thank you for showing me to my rooms, but I think, perhaps if the lady wouldn't be opposed, we could take a promenade outside and remember our old adventures? And you can tell me about this play. I'm sorry to have missed it."

The earl grinned. "There will be a warm fire awaiting your return. Mariah, sweetling, don't forget your gloves this time, mm?"

A few minutes later, both clad in their outerwear, they slid out a side door into the dormant gardens. A few flurries were still falling, though not enough to add to the whisper of snowfall clinging to the grass. He found himself hoping more would come over the next few days so that they could bring out the sleigh—he had a lovely memory of a sleigh ride on his first visit.

They walked in silence for a few moments. Each step of it made him a little less certain of what he wanted to say. It had been easy enough inside, with her family, when he'd slipped back into the role he'd taken on twelve years ago—her defender. But now? Out here? Just the two of them?

She came to a sudden stop at the garden's edge and spun to face him. Given the look on her face, he braced himself, though he wasn't certain exactly what form her barrage would take.

"I want to get something clear here and now," she said, standing straight as a peppermint stick. "I only mean to be your friend. I don't have any foolish notions about—you know." She fluttered a gloved hand. "Keeping the manor in the family by marrying you just because it's convenient. But having a brain, as you do, you'll have considered that we've considered it."

He had. And he'd been conflicted, not knowing which Mariah they'd be trying to convince him to marry—the childhood friend or the stranger she'd become. But then when Pearl had suggested it, hinting that it was the only reason anyone would marry him . . . well, that had made the whole suggestion seem wretched.

He granted Mariah's point with a tilt of his head.

She went on. "I know—I know about Lady Pearl. And what's more, I have no desire to marry for convenience. So let's just dismiss that now, all right? I'm not setting my cap for you. I only want to be your friend."

His lips twitched. Did she have any idea how sweet she looked with that embarrassed determination on her face? Probably not. "There isn't much to know about Lady Pearl. But even so, your stance is noted."

She whooshed out a breath. "Good. Friends, then?"

"Well, I don't know. That rather depends, doesn't it?"

Her pretty chestnut brows drew together. "On what?"

Hands clasped behind his back, he leaned a little closer. "On why the Mariah I thought I knew so well vanished these last several years."

For a second, horror flashed in her eyes—chased by amusement. "The letters? Mama decided she had better oversee them once I turned fifteen."

Never once had the thought crossed his mind before . . . but it made sense, now that he realized that his old friend was still very much there within her grown-up form. He clucked his tongue. "And you didn't sneak any real ones out?"

"I tried." She laughed at whatever memory that brought up. "I had no idea of your direction. Mama or Papa always put them in the post. And apparently the postman needs more than 'Cyril, probably at Oxford soon' to deliver a letter."

He laughed too, more ancient fears flying away. With exaggerated gallantry, he offered his arm. "Well, my lady, there is no postmaster necessary now. And a fairy world ahead. Tell me, is the Almond Gate still intact?"

Her smile would have rivaled the sun in August and certainly put its wintry face to shame. "Of course." She held out the page, filled front and back with a tiny, sloppy scrawl in two different hands. "And Christmas Wood waits beyond it."

He took the page, she took his arm, and they set off toward the copse of trees. "Christmas Wood, Orange Creek, and . . . what did we call the lake?"

"Orgeat." She closed her eyes, as if in delight at the thought of the almond syrup.

He could relate. "Orgeat. I haven't had any decent orgeat in years."

"You'll have some now. And mincemeat pies and marzipan figures and gingerbread men—"

"And peppermint sticks and candied almonds and—"

"Sugar plums!" they pronounced together, exchanging smiles.

Cyril couldn't decide, as they followed the path toward the wood, if he felt ten again . . . or if perhaps, for the first time in his adult life, he simply felt how he should.

Hopeful.

5

$\mathcal{S}$øren Gyldenkrone stood still as a statue, ignoring both the bustle of the train depot and his brother's infernal pacing. Rage in his blood wasn't a hot and pulsing thing—it was a slow, steady, ice-cold thrum that sharpened his focus and pushed peripheral things into neat alignment, to be looked at only when they could be useful.

He'd spent the last week with this same icy focus, slicing through each and every one of his brother's excuses. Trying—and failing—to tamp down the gossip, working relentlessly to fix what Emil, in his idiocy, had broken.

As usual.

Thrum. Thrum. Thrum.

He could hear the cold fury coursing through him, feel its chill in his limbs. This time, when his brother paced in front of him, he snapped, "Do stop."

He spoke in Danish, which he only did when he and Emil were alone. It was rude, otherwise, and he was never rude. When in England, one spoke English. When in France, one spoke French. To deliberately confuse the people around him or keep them in the dark as to his meaning was absolutely inappropriate.

Emil forgot *that* half the time, too, and constantly instigated conversations in their native tongue instead of that of the nation they were visiting. It made him a tiresome traveling companion, truth be told.

But he was his brother. His only brother. They two were the only Gyldenkrones left in the world, their noble family name in danger of extinction if they didn't soon select wives and set about producing the next generation.

Søren had been ready to marry a year ago. Ingrid would have been a perfect wife in many ways. But when the king asked one to choose an English bride instead, one obeyed one's monarch and cousin. When the Crown Prince promised that a match would be made between one of his own children and whatever child one produced with said English bride, one bowed one's head in honor and thanked him for deeming one worthy.

Politics had been the milk on which he'd been raised. He understood it, relished it, took his strength from it. He knew well why this favor was asked—tensions between England and Germany grew colder with each passing year, and Denmark's ties to Germany were solid. Dangerously solid. She needed equally strong ties to England if she intended to maintain the neutrality on which she prided herself. But the Crown Prince had long ago married Alexandrine in Canne, and future royals would choose other royals from Europe's ruling families to wed. The chance to form an alliance directly with England simply hadn't worked out, generationally speaking.

But cousins were glorious things. As one of the most influential families in Denmark, Søren could do for his king what the prince himself couldn't. He could choose a wife from an equally prominent family in England. A family that was not of the crown itself but that was respected by the king. Beloved.

The perfect match.

His fingers tightened on the silver head of his cane, carried solely for fashion and not any other use. He rubbed his thumb over the familiar engraving—the Danish lion that adorned their

national coat of arms, borrowed from the crest of their most fa-
mous king, Christian V.

Emil had paused his pacing, at least, but now he stood before
Søren with his arms crossed over his chest, glowering. Søren lifted
one brow, solely because he knew his brother couldn't mimic him,
much as he'd tried to teach himself the gesture. His facial muscles
never cooperated.

Emil dropped his arms and gusted out a breath. "I want to
come with you."

"No." Søren lifted one hand from the head of his cane, fished
inside his pocket, and pulled out his watch. Three minutes until
his private train car ought to be ready. Ten until the train would
leave the station, on its way to Derbyshire. "You were not invited."

"Neither were you!"

Søren flinched at the very insinuation that he had done something so base. "Of course I was. Lord Castleton was quite clear
that I was welcome to pay him a visit absolutely any time—and
he also made a point of telling me how charming his home is at
Christmastide."

Emil fumed like a steam vent. "It isn't fair. I'm the one that prat
Lightbourne embarrassed. I deserve the chance to—"

"You deserve?" He speared his brother with a hard glance.
"What you deserve is to be left to restore your own tarnished honor.
If it wouldn't be a blot on our entire family, I would do just that.
You ought to be thanking me for cleaning up after your mess, yet
again."

"Thanking you," Emil muttered, spinning to pace again. "It's
your fault I found myself in the situation to begin with."

"My fault?" Søren laughed, though there was no amusement in
it, and even his hardheaded brother couldn't mistake it for that.
"Oh yes. I am the one who makes you constantly run off at the
mouth. I am the one constantly urging you to resort to fists instead
of diplomacy. I am the one—"

"You were the one actually considering marriage to that scheming little poppet!" Emil stopped again before him, lifting a hand so he could poke a finger into Søren's shoulder.

One would have thought he'd have been broken of that habit ages ago, given the many times Søren had done exactly what he did now—knock his hand away with one swift, snapping motion of his cane.

As always, Emil cursed and shook out his smarting finger. And yet no doubt he'd do the same thing next month.

Søren set his cane back on the pavement with a satisfying click. "Lady Pearl can scheme all she likes. It was her family I was considering, not her childish antics. If I were to decide she suited my needs, she would have to agree to my stipulations. Nothing forces a girl to grow up faster than taking on the responsibilities of a foreign household."

"And you call me the idiot. She'd never be faithful to you. The very fact that she was toying with that blighter—and that she didn't reject me—should have told you that."

It had indeed been disturbing to learn that the lady hadn't pushed away his brother's advances. He could admit that. It was part of the ice in his veins. Infidelity was even more shameful than Emil's constant pursuit of diversions above responsibility.

But she was young. And Emil was charming, when he tried to be. And he and Pearl hadn't even been engaged yet, much less married. Kissing another man wasn't to her credit, but it wasn't unfaithfulness, exactly.

He would have made it clear that if they wed, any other flirtations must stop immediately. It ought to go without saying, but he wasn't naïve. He knew it didn't always.

When he'd calmly confronted her about it, she hadn't been repentant, though. More put out that he dared to be upset with her instead of his brother.

He hadn't bothered explaining that he was always upset with his brother. It was the baseline of life and had been since they were boys. He'd come to grips long ago with the fact that his brother was a selfish creature, but that some of his most reckless acts were, in his way of thinking, done for the benefit of others.

This was a perfect example. Every single time Søren had considered courting a woman, Emil took it upon himself to see if her heart was true. If she could be lured away by Emil's charms, then she wasn't suited to becoming Søren's wife.

Ingrid had resisted. Pearl had not.

Part of him appreciated the test, even as the greater part wanted to lock his brother in a tower somewhere until he'd outgrown his childishness. He'd always wanted whatever Søren had. Had always tried to snatch it away. Horses, toys, friends, and now ladies. It was just Emil, much as he wished it weren't.

Right on time, the steward opened the door to the private car he'd rented and bowed to him. "All is ready to your specifications, my lord."

"Thank you." English emerged from his lips as easily as the Danish had moments before. He started forward.

Emil jumped into his way. "At least tell me your intentions." He still spoke in Danish, despite the steward now within hearing.

As if telling his brother his intentions didn't guarantee that he'd find a way to interfere and ruin everything. Again. "To buff out the tarnish you've given our family's honor. That's all you need to know." English still, though low enough that the steward probably couldn't hear them. He was polite, not stupid.

"Søren."

"Try to stay out of trouble while I'm gone, Emil." He once again lifted his cane, this time using it like an arm to urge his brother aside. Gently but firmly. "In fact, you really *ought* to go ahead home. Enjoy the holiday with your friends. I'll follow in the new year, and I'll have my bride-to-be with me."

Emil's face screwed into a pout in the exact way he'd done since he was a toddler. "At least tell me it's not Pearl. I don't think I could tolerate her as a sister-in-law."

As if that was a deciding factor. But he could grant his brother that much. "There are other families just as esteemed by King Edward—and whose daughters are less conniving."

Lady Mariah Lyons had always been one of his top contenders, and the fact that a visit to her family now would also give him the opportunity to put Cyril Lightbourne in his place might as well have been a finger from heaven pointing the way to satisfaction.

"Good." It was the relief in his tone that did it—that always did it. That made Søren love him, despite not liking him half the time. "She's not good enough for you."

And that too. Huffing out an exasperated breath, Søren clapped a hand to his brother's shoulder. "Go home, brother. Enjoy some *racine* and *risalamande* for me."

Emil smiled, the petulance replaced by genuine cheer. "I think I will, at that. As long as you promise to tell me about your revenge on the blighter." He lifted a hand to touch the abrasions on his face.

Suddenly glad that his brother still hadn't reverted to English, Søren nodded. "In the new year."

"In the new year."

He moved into his train car as his brother strode back toward their carriage, content that Emil wouldn't follow him to Castleton. He didn't really care if he returned to Copenhagen or stayed in London, so long as he didn't come to Castleton to have a rematch with Cyril Lightbourne.

Søren had witnessed the brawl, though he'd tried to remain out of sight. His brother didn't stand a chance, even if he had the good sense to pick his next fight when he was fully sober. Whoever trained Lightbourne had done a better job than Emil's instructor. Or, more likely, Lightbourne had been a better student.

Though he could handle himself and a weapon if necessary, Søren had no intention of challenging "the blighter" as Emil would do. He would never endanger relations between their two countries by actually hurting a prominent citizen. And besides, exchanging fisticuffs—even besting him at them—wouldn't set anything to rights.

No. Cyril Lightbourne had smudged the Gyldenkrone family honor, and he would pay for it in kind. He had done it for the sake of an undeserving woman, and perhaps that would play a part in Søren's recompense.

He didn't know his exact plan yet. Only his tactic. The details would fall into place just as they always did as he gathered information and took in the lay of the land. All he knew right now was that he intended to ruin whatever Lightbourne esteemed most highly. Tarnish it just as he had so blithely tarnished the Gyldenkrone reputation.

And he'd accomplish that on the side, while he fulfilled his duty to his cousins and convinced Lady Mariah to marry him.

As the train chugged out of the station right on schedule, Søren relaxed in his richly upholstered chair and drew his leatherbound journal from his inner coat pocket. He had better refresh himself now on their previous meetings. Families were always impressed when he could recall names and situations and ask them insightful questions.

When was it that he had met the noble side of the Lightbourne family? June. Mid-June. In the height of the Season, at . . . yes, that was right. The Middletons' ball. He flipped to the appropriate page in his journal and reread the notes he had taken down that evening, as he did at the close of every day.

He'd listed every new acquaintance to whom he'd been introduced, along with his impressions of them. Each young lady with whom he'd danced, and about what they had spoken. Each previous acquaintance with whom he'd had a conversation, and on what topic.

Halfway down the list he saw Lord Geoffrey Lightbourne, Earl of Castleton, and his wife, Lady Beatrice Lightbourne, formerly Lady Lyons. Her son, Lord Frederic Lyons, Viscount, and her youngest daughter, Lady Mariah Lyons. One elder daughter, widowed, not in attendance.

He read his physical descriptions of them all, his notes about their preferred names or nicknames—Castleton or Cass for the earl, and Lyons for the viscount, though his family called him Fred. And his impressions—that the earl and countess were pleasant and amiable and among the favorites of London society. That the earl was a regular companion of King Edward whenever they were both in town and even visited each other's country homes at least once a year—that was crucial. He was not quite the intimate of the king that Lord Kingeland was, hence his stepdaughter's rank as second on his list, but close enough.

That Lyons was a reasonable enough chap, his head firmly attached to his shoulders. And that the daughter, Lady Mariah, was her brother's opposite. Her head was filled with fluff rather than reason, and though she didn't speak often at the ball, when she did, it was utter rot. She was pretty enough, he'd noted, and seemed good-natured, which was important. Silly, not conniving.

That was something. Silliness could be corrected far more easily. And really, *corrected* wasn't even the word for it. Silliness tended to fall by the wayside in the face of household responsibilities, children, and the pressures of court. What Lady Mariah was, was young. Too young, in some ways, but that too would correct itself in time.

A corner of his mouth twitched up a bit at that. She'd made his thirty-one years feel ancient, yes, as had Lady Pearl. But twelve years was no great thing between adults. His own father had been thirteen years his mother's senior, and it had never caused any problems. Even Prince Christian and Princess Alexandrine were nine years apart, and their three years of marriage thus far had been happy enough.

He paused, checked another note, and let out a relieved breath. Yes, he had remembered to post a gift to the princess in plenty of time for it to arrive before her Christmas Eve birthday. He'd thought so, but it never hurt to double-check.

Thumbing back to his notes from the summer, including his two visits to the Lightbourne London home, he finished up those and then skipped ahead to September. The Lightbourne-Lyons family had departed—and only then, interestingly enough, did Mr. Cyril Lightbourne arrive in London.

He'd wondered then why the heir apparent had seemingly avoided his benefactor, and he wondered it again now. Something to be discovered, yes. To be exploited? Perhaps.

As fate would have it, he'd crossed paths with "the blighter" only days after he reached Town—when he'd somehow finagled his way into Lady Pearl's graces. Oh, he'd heard the story about the heroism, but that couldn't actually be what caught the lady's eye. She was too dedicated to her scheming for that. No, more likely was that she'd realized he stood to inherit the Castleton estate, which she would know was beyond compare. *That* was what would have caught her attention.

Søren hadn't been worried. A relative so distant could always be displaced by a miraculous child, or even a closer cousin coming out of the woodwork. And besides, his own holdings in Denmark compared favorably, and his title was the equivalent. More, he had that promise of Prince Christian that had spurred him here. And what ambitious young lady wouldn't prize the idea of her child becoming a prince or princess? Perhaps even the Crown Princess, if births worked out appropriately?

He'd known that Lightbourne was no real threat to his court. Emil, on the other hand . . .

And that was where things spiraled. Emil thought it his duty to sound out Pearl's fidelity. She had failed the test—disappointing, but not especially surprising. She was, above all, a conceited creature. She would have looked lovely on his arm in the Danish court, yes, but he hadn't been entirely convinced she had a personality compatible with Princess Alexandrine's, and that was crucial. Otherwise, he would have proposed months ago.

But her indiscretion could have remained private, had Emil not gotten drunk at the Marlborough a week ago and bragged about his conquest. And had Lightbourne not been there with a friend of his and heard it. And had he not taken it upon himself to defend Lady Pearl's besmirched honor.

Even then, it wouldn't have been so bad had he not trounced Emil so handily, and had every single aristocrat left in London not been there that night for a holiday party. And had his brother then had the sense to stay down, it would have been little more than one in a long line of minor humiliations. Most of the gentlemen there had lost a brawl when they'd overindulged, he'd wager.

But no. Emil had staggered up. Said something about Pearl deserving no better than the likes of Lightbourne. And Lightbourne had done the unforgivable. He'd insulted the entire Gyldenkrone line by saying that no real gentleman would ever act as Emil had.

"Perhaps such disrespect is common in Denmark," he'd said, *"but it isn't to be borne in England."*

Utter rot, of course—gentlemen behaved in that exact way all the time, in England as often as anywhere else in Europe. But to insinuate that his brother was baseborn—and then, worse, to call the moral fiber of Denmark into question?

No. That was intolerable. He could never forgive himself if he let that slight to his king and country go unanswered.

He'd said nothing that night. He'd slipped away, unnoticed by most of the crowd. But he'd known then that he would have to do something to discredit the idealistic young buck. Something to make everyone either chuckle and write him off or turn away in disgust. Even better if he could make sure it stung him to the core, as his words had done to Søren. He would have to be careful, however—if he meant to claim Lady Mariah as his bride, he couldn't besmirch her stepfather's name, only that distant cousin's.

But Søren was nothing if not careful.

He closed his journal after that, leaned back in his chair, and closed his eyes. It would be best if he arrived at Plumford Manor well-rested and mentally sharp, all his observational skills at the ready.

Morning had turned to afternoon by the time the train chugged into his stop, and he disembarked. As promised, the Castleton carriage awaited him, and he climbed in with a nod to the footman holding the door open for him. They passed quickly through the small village of Hope, where the railway station was, drove what couldn't be more than a mile or two to Castleton and through it, along the road into the countryside, and soon were through the gates of Plumford Manor.

He could appreciate what he saw—the beautiful countryside, the cleverly braided hedgerows, and the stately manor. He did indeed hope he'd have a chance to explore a bit of the High Peaks while he was here. He knew Christian would appreciate any descriptions he brought home.

What made him smile the moment he set his feet to the frosty ground, however, was the fact that Lady Mariah came laughing around the corner of the house even then . . . arm in arm with Mr. Cyril Lightbourne himself. Lightbourne, who smiled down at the lady with rapt attention and unmistakable adoration.

Oh, this was going to be almost too easy. Two birds . . . one lightly lobbed stone. And he'd have his revenge and his bride in one fell swoop.

6

Mariah's carefree morning came crashing down around her the moment she rounded the house on Cyril's arm and saw the greve standing there. The last thirty-six hours had been simple and carefree, her parents' expectations happily shoved aside in the light of her truce with Cyril. With that understanding between them, they'd been free to reminisce and laugh and get caught up on the years since they'd fallen out of touch. Last night, she, Cyril, and Papa had stayed up long into the night, roasting chestnuts and talking about absolutely everything, and she'd awakened this morning grateful for how *easy* it was to simply be Cyril's friend again.

But there was nothing easy or simple or carefree about Lord Gyldenkrone. He was exactly as she remembered him—tall, chiseled, golden, and so very handsome. He looked like some modernized representation of a Nordic god—both in good looks and in that stoic demeanor carved from ice. It wasn't that he ever came across as cruel or hard in that sense. Just . . . controlled. Calculating. That was the impression she'd always gotten from him. That his every move, his every word, his every thought was a careful calculation—and that he was just as carefully scrutinizing every motion of every person around him.

As romantic a picture as he struck, and as compelling a story as he told, and as much as the unmarried women in London had been abuzz about him, he was quite intimidating. The two times he'd come to call in Town, Mariah's hands had shaken the entire time. Her mind, on the other hand, had whirred. He looked as though he ought to be wearing some Viking outfit. A cloak made of wolf pelt. Carrying a broadsword.

Instead, he wore an expensive, perfectly tailored suit of clothes, and today it was topped with a heavy woolen overcoat and stylish fedora.

She half expected it to sprout Viking horns at any moment.

His all-seeing gaze homed in on them in half an instant, and she felt the weight of it like a block of ice, sending a shiver down her spine. The smile he offered looked at once like it always did—chilly perfection—and yet somehow not. It was undoubtedly only her overactive imagination that made images of white arctic wolves spring to mind.

Probably.

She ought to say something, but the only thing she could think of was an apology, and she wasn't even sure what it was for. Being out here when he arrived and hence ruining the careful welcome they'd have ready indoors? For being found lacking with the first sweep of his gaze? For suddenly wishing he'd opted to spend Christmas with some other family of some other eligible young lady?

Not that she wasn't flattered—and not that she was opposed to getting to know him—but that singular gaze of his reminded her in a heartbeat that if Gyldenkrone was here, there would be nothing simple and easy about the holiday. It wouldn't be all carefree joy and reminiscence of childhood.

It would be one prolonged interview in which she was certain to come up lacking a dozen times over.

Before she could form her lips around any words, he spoke, even as the massive front doors—both again!—swung open. "Ah,

Lady Mariah. I cannot express how glad I am to be welcomed among your esteemed family this holiday season. You are, as ever, looking lovely."

Her cheeks were no doubt already pink from the cold, but now they flushed with heat. "Welcome, my lord," she finally managed to squeak out, though she sounded like little more than a mouse. As she always did in a crowded ballroom, keenly aware that none of the masses swarming her cared a whit what she thought. That they'd laugh—or frown, like Lord Gyldenkrone had done—if she dared to answer any questions honestly.

"What did you think of the regatta this morning?"

"Oh, I pretended they were invading Vikings and we were the first Britons to spot them, not sure if they were friend or foe."

Frown.

"You attended the musicale last evening, did you not? Wasn't the baritone divine?"

"Indeed! As he sang, I couldn't dislodge the images from Shakespeare's A Midsummer Night's Dream *from my mind and was trying to cast the attendees in the roles. Who do you think should be Titania?"*

Frown.

That last one she'd thought for sure would be acceptable. Shakespeare! Who could take issue with Shakespeare?

Gyldenkrone, apparently.

Papa rushed down the steps, his eyes shouting all sorts of warnings at her that only made her heart sink lower, barely covered up by the smile he beamed at their new guest. "Ah, my lord! How do you do? So glad to have you with us."

In one fluid motion, Gyldenkrone looked to Papa and held out a hand, transferring his silver-headed walking stick to his left hand for the exchange. "Very well, thank you. And I trust you are too? Your lovely stepdaughter certainly looks to be the picture of perfect health." He glanced her way again, those ice-blue eyes as compelling and, she was sure, as dangerous as a fjord.

Fjords were dangerous, right? When covered in ice?

She should have brushed up on her Scandinavian knowledge before their guest arrived.

"Yes, quite," Papa was saying, clearly not afraid of plunging through the ice into some treacherous fjord. "Have you been introduced to Mr. Lightbourne?"

"Yes." One word. One syllable. A world of meaning so intricately layered that Mariah hadn't a hope of sorting them all.

She frowned. Because what came through loud and clear was that Gyldenkrone didn't much like Cyril. And from the way Cyril had gone stiff as a stone, the feeling was mutual.

"Indeed," Cyril replied. "At the Kingelands.'"

Mariah felt her own muscles turn to stone too. It had been easy to let herself forget about Lady Pearl. What part could she play, after all, in the world of recollection Mariah had been living in for the past thirty-six hours? Pearl hadn't been there as Mariah and Cyril laughed their way through their old adventure story, nor had she huddled around the roaring hearth with them and Papa later. She hadn't been a part of the wandering, wonderful conversation last night, nor at the breakfast table with them this morning. She certainly hadn't been present as Cyril again offered Mariah his arm and led her back into what they'd long ago dubbed Christmas Wood, in search of the ancient, gnarled tree they'd forgotten to look for yesterday.

But it seemed that with Gyldenkrone's arrival, Lady Pearl had invaded too.

Papa sent her a look she couldn't quite decipher. Concerned? Chiding? Silently telling her to pull herself together and put a little effort into freeing one or another of these men from Pearl's talons?

She sighed. One couldn't call her and Pearl *rivals*. That implied there was competition. There had never been any. Pearl had beaten her out at absolutely everything at school without as much as a glance her way; Pearl had gathered the other young ladies as friends, leaving but a few sprinkled outcasts to wander about alone, like Mariah had done. And Pearl had then debuted to such great success that it had left no one to even notice the likes of her.

Now, somehow, she had even invaded Mariah's Christmas, thanks to these two men vying for Pearl's favor. Never mind that they were both *here*. That wasn't because of Mariah, not really. It was because of Papa. If it weren't for him, neither of these gents would have ever spared her a word or a glance.

Papa turned his smile back to the Dane. "Then we can skip the introductions—excellent. You must be worn from your travel, my lord. Please, won't you come inside? We have tea ready, and our best suite prepared for you in the bachelor wing."

"The trip was quite comfortable, actually. Though I will be delighted to partake of your hospitality. As long as Lady Mariah will be joining us?"

He turned his lips up into a perfect, handsome smile. Perfect, handsome, but still it felt as warm as an arctic wind. Was it because of whatever rivalry he had with Cyril? His lack of feeling toward her? Or was she being unfair? Perhaps it was simply his way, and it was her imagination that had her ascribing such chill-wracked words to it.

Regardless, she couldn't let either of these guests deter her from the real task today. "I'll be in directly, my lord. I must check on Professor Skylark first." Upon this, she gave Papa her sweetest smile. "He sent me a note this morning, asking me to come by his workshop before luncheon."

Papa narrowed his eyes a bit, but he had too much respect for his old tutor to ever contradict his requests. "Of course. But don't dally, sweetling. You don't want to keep Lord Gyldenkrone waiting overlong for your company."

Gyldenkrone sent another handsome, frosty smile her way. "No need to rush, my lady. It is my goal that we shall enjoy . . . end-less opportunity to become better acquainted. And frankly, Lord Castleton, I would request a private meeting with you first."

His implications were clear, as sharp and pointed as his gaze. Mariah found herself fighting to work breath into her lungs.

He couldn't be serious. He couldn't mean to ask Papa here and now for permission to court her—or more. He couldn't mean that he intended to spend the rest of his life with her. It made no sense. He didn't even like her! He'd wanted Lady Pearl, not Mariah, like everyone else. And yet his gaze lingered now on *her*, those clear-as-ice words hanging there in the air between them.

Then crisp air filled her lungs and clarity her mind. He'd come to England to find a bride whose family was close to King Edward. And she boasted two such families. She had both the dowry left to her by her late father and a too-generous promised addition from Papa. She had both a brother already a viscount and a stepfather who was an earl. She knew well those connections were all he cared about. She didn't know why he'd struck Pearl from his list, but he was obviously making his decisions based on things other than affection.

She had no reason to feel such a pang over it. No reason to feel the Christmas joy seep out of her heart as she realized that the motivation of these two bachelors were both naught but convenience and political decisions.

That's what *she* would be. A sound choice. A reasonable decision. Perhaps even someone to be settled for when the more alluring option fell through.

Mariah's shoulders sagged.

At the Dane's words, Papa beamed like the summer sun and held out an arm in invitation. "I'll let the rest of the family welcome you first—and I don't believe you've met Mariah's elder sister yet—but then you and I shall adjourn to my study."

Mariah mustered up a smile for them and put cheer—false, but necessary—back into place.

Cyril led her around the carriage now pulling round to the back where the greve's trunks and bags would be unloaded, and then off into the southern garden, since that was where they'd been aiming before. He'd yet to actually see the outbuilding assigned to Professor Skylark as his workshop to know where to lead her specifically, but she took over once they were on the garden path.

Cyril frowned the moment their feet touched the paving stones. "Please tell me you don't mean to entertain his suit."

"I'd never honestly considered he meant to bring one. But why do you say that?" She sent a glance over her shoulder, a bit of her usual spirit creeping back in. "He isn't *really* going to shift into an arctic wolf and devour us all, nor break out his Viking weapons, I daresay."

Cyril laughed, but it didn't last long. "He's far too measured to allow his inner wolf to show itself in society. You only need to fear if he lures you out in the wilds."

She breathed a laugh too. "But the serious question?"

He sighed. "He isn't good enough for you, that's all. Not noble enough of spirit. He certainly doesn't deserve to figure as the hero in your story."

Her brows felt as though they were trying to leap straight off her forehead. "Are you quite serious? He's . . ." She waved a hand back toward the house, searching for the right words. "Well, cold, obviously. But in that way that puts nobility and uprightness above all. You can fault his lack of affection, but I don't know how you would dare to fault his nobility."

Rather than answer, Cyril clenched his teeth.

Ah. This wasn't really about Gyldenkrone's nature, and it certainly wasn't about Mariah. It was about Pearl. She attempted to twist it into a tease, even if the words felt flat on her tongue. "I do believe you're just sore because he's a rival for Lady Pearl's affections."

"Affections?" Something strange traveled over his face, then vanished again. "I don't think affection is what she felt for Gyldenkrone. Ambition . . . yes. He sorely tempted her ambitions. Honestly, I thought she was his choice and he hers—no offense intended toward you."

She just barely held back another sigh. Drew out another practiced smile, like Mama had taught her do. "The Kingelands are a prominent family, and she's far more beautiful than I am. If those qualities are what he desires, then I admit I'm confused as to why he's even here." *Unless* . . . She darted a look at Cyril.

Unless Pearl had told him that she'd made her choice for Cyril. Unless "practically engaged" was soon to become "actually engaged." Unless Gyldenkrone had been convinced enough that he called a retreat and resorted to the runner-up on his list of bridal candidates.

Cyril was glancing over his shoulder, his look contemplative, rather than at her face, which no doubt revealed more than she'd want it to. "You don't give yourself enough credit, Ri. Though even so, I admit to sharing your confusion. When I left London, I was all but certain they'd be engaged before I could return."

He was clearly better than she was at masking his disappointment. He said it evenly, cooly—no doubt a result of too much practice making certain his heart wasn't pinned to his sleeve when in the company of Pearl's plethora of suitors.

She lifted her chin, trying to remember Mama's lessons in how to achieve that very thing herself. One would think she'd be an old hand at it by now, having always come in second or third—or tenth. "Well, you ought to be thanking us both then, I suppose. If he decides on me, that removes one of your prime rivals for Lady Pearl's hand."

Cyril sent her a look she couldn't quite decipher, and she hadn't much time to try to do so anyway. In the next moment, a loud crash sounded from up ahead, in the professor's workshop. Eyes wide, she abandoned Cyril's arm altogether so she could lift her skirts and dash toward the building.

"Professor?" she called as she neared the door. She wrenched it open, her eyes flying over the crammed space. "Are you all right?"

"Quite, quite." His voice, however, came from under a mound

of cardpaper boxes that were spilling little wooden toys onto the floor. "Just a small avalanche. No damage done but to the order."

Order was a bit of an exaggeration on a good day, and an utter misnomer in the days leading up to Christmas. She waded through some of the detritus so she could move enough of the boxes to reveal his face.

He was grinning, which meant he couldn't be injured. But his wig was askew, his spectacles dangling from one ear, and he was on his rear end on the floor. She frowned even as she held out her hand. "You fell."

"Nonsense. I merely sat . . . in an unplanned fashion. And wheeled my arms, which is what caused the avalanche." Back on his feet, though knee-high in boxes, he looked about him, patting his pockets. "Now where have my spectacles got to?"

She reached over, gently unhooking them from his ear and handing them back to him so he could position them correctly on his prominent nose.

He beamed, and it only grew when he looked beyond her. "Ah! This must be Mr. Lightbourne! How do you do, good sir, how do you do?"

They exchanged pleasantries, brief due to the obvious awe on Cyril's face as he took in the workshop. "Forgive me," he said after the niceties were through, "but this looks quite intriguing."

Professor Skylark smiled wide and waded out of the fallen boxes. "Doesn't it just? Toys, nearly all of it. There is nothing in the world like bringing a child joy, you know."

Mariah bent down, pulled one of the wooden figures from where it had fallen from its box, and handed it to Cyril with a small smile that felt self-conscious on her lips.

His eyes lit. "It's a nutcracker!"

"Modeled on Lady Mariah's most prized possession," the professor said, obviously not realizing who had given it to her. She knew, though, and so did Cyril, which meant that heat stung her cheeks again. "A miniature but fully functional model, appropriate

70

only for the smallest of nuts. But the village children adore them. We create a new variation each year—proud hussars for the little lads and noble ladies for the lasses."

He stooped and pulled out a female version of the toy. This one had a long dress instead of legs, but the same short cape that acted as the lever controlling her jaw. This year, both hussars and ladies were dressed in royal purple, gold paint bringing light and life to each tiny decoration on their clothes—buttons and trim and intricate designs.

Cyril took the female one too, his face awash with awe as he moved their fully articulated limbs and bent them at the waist and back up. "And you've made these? By hand?"

"Well of course! What else would an old, tired tutor do with his time?" Professor Skylark smiled happily and motioned to his workbench, which took up a large portion of the room. "I spend all year on them, and on the grand display for the Christmas Eve Ball. Which is what I requested your help with, my dear Lady Mariah."

She followed his motioning hand into the back corner of the workshop—the only part even a little bit tidy. Her eager glance was soon disappointed, though. Though bits and pieces of mechanisms sat out, she had no idea what they would be put together into. "Still being mysterious, I see. Not even a hint for your favorite pupil, Professor?"

Professor Skylark chuckled and darted here and there, pulling bits and baubles from his vast array of shelves. "And miss the delight on your face when we unveil it in the house this evening? Never! But I do require your opinion." He held out two small figures, both made of a combination of wood, metal, and cloth. Both made with the same detail and attention he always gave his creations. Both depictions of men.

They both boasted brown hair in varying shades, with the true difference marked by the colors of their clothing. One wore pale crystal blue, the other a deep purple.

He danced them both back and forth, one in either hand. "One must be the hero of my little visual story, the other the villain. Which should be which, do you think?"

She smiled, looking from one to the other. Both were handsome miniatures, and both had faces painted without much expression, so that the children could imagine whatever they wanted upon it. But the purple matched the other nutcracker dolls, so she tapped it. "Hero."

The professor made a show of studying her for a moment, in the way that she imagined he'd done when giving Papa an oral quiz. "Quite certain? Once I attach them to their tracks, it will be difficult to change."

"No question in my mind."

"So be it." His favorite enigmatic smile making happy wrinkles in his cheeks, Professor Skylark turned to put the figures back in their cubbies. "Now then. I don't suppose you could spare a few more moments to, ah . . . ?" He motioned toward the mess by the door.

Mariah laughed and turned that way again. "I would be delighted to assist, Professor."

"I could get lost in here all day, I think." Cyril dragged his gaze back from the cuckoo clock he'd been studying, its innards in pieces on the bench, and moved to the tumble of boxes too.

It would take an hour, at least, to put the toys back inside their containers. And maybe, if she smiled just so, the professor would let her help tie the boxes with ribbon, rather than insisting she get back to whatever duties awaited her inside. An hour, maybe two or three, before she would go back into the house and learn what the greve had said to her father.

Call her a coward, but she would take the reprieve.

7

*C*yril gripped his fork too tightly, especially considering that he had no intention of lifting another bite to his lips. How could he, when to admit its entrance he'd have to unclench his jaw? That had proven more and more difficult as the meal wore on.

He'd thought, when Mariah told him about her previous encounters with Gyldenkrone on their slow walk back from the professor's workshop, that she must be exaggerating his cool response to her. She obviously thought of herself in terms not nearly glowing enough—even in the scant time they'd been together again, he'd picked up on that. She had claimed no fewer than a half-dozen times to have been an utter failure during the Season, and he just couldn't fathom it.

How could the London gents not be knocking down Castleton's door in search of her attention? She was lovely and clever and altogether charming—one never knew what bit of whimsy might next fall from her lips, and awaiting the discovery had become his new favorite pastime.

Gyldenkrone, however, didn't seem to share his amusement. He met her every sentence with a frown of his fair brows and with even, careful words that didn't exactly put her down but certainly didn't lift her up. If this man truly wanted to marry her, shouldn't he be smiling over her wit? Laughing in delight at her imagination? Looking at her with appreciation, not just calculation?

It proved what Cyril already knew about him—he was more statue than man. Made of ice rather than flesh. A man willing to let his brother insult the woman he'd been about to propose to couldn't be trusted to properly care for any other woman either.

Mariah was currently studying her plate, scooting her spears of asparagus back and forth without tasting them. He could all but hear her mentally chanting to herself, *Be what they expect, just be what they expect.*

It wasn't right.

Gyldenkrone had noted her subdued behavior as well. He put on a smile, yes. But his tone was lacking genuine curiosity as he asked, "Do you not care for asparagus, my lady?"

She paused. Set down her fork. Looked up toward, but not at, the greve. And seemed to ruminate for a long moment on what she could say. "I do. But I find myself not very hungry."

Lady Castleton had positioned them around the table, and while last night Cyril had been beside Mariah, tonight he'd been put across from her, Gyldenkrone at her side. Louise was to Cyril's left, directly across from the greve. She frowned at her sister. "It is sinful to waste food when so many are hungry."

Gyldenkrone nodded once. "Very true. Having plenty is no excuse to waste the gifts God has given us."

Mariah's larynx bobbed. "I assure you, I do not make a habit of waste—and I *do* make a habit of giving to those in need."

Cyril's smile felt more forced than the seating arrangement. "Do you still walk through the neighborhood on Boxing Day to make certain the village children have sweets enough?"

Louise huffed an unamused laugh. "A rather silly interpretation of St. Stephen's Day, though it was endearing when she was a child. We eventually had to convince her that real food and alms would do them more good than leftover gingerbread and sugar plums."

Gyldenkrone's smile soured Cyril's mood even more. "It speaks to a worthy spirit in a child, though. Just as it speaks to a worthy family to hone the instinct into practicality."

Mariah winced a bit at the word *practicality*. Of course she *knew* what was practical—that a family that hadn't enough bread didn't need confections as much as staples.

But at the same time, when else would they get the sugar plums and gingerbread?

His fingers tightened around his fork again. His family had never been destitute—but when his father was alive, the man had been so stingy with Cyril and Mother that there was never anything *but* the practical things for them. No money given for sweet treats or toys. He saw that their needs were met—and nothing more.

He could still remember standing outside the window of a bakery, wondering what those confections tasted like. Father didn't like sweets—so none were permitted in the house. Father didn't like music—so none sang its way through their rooms. Father didn't like the sound of Cyril's laughter or the sight of him curled up with a book instead of being outside "like a proper lad," so anytime the man was home, Cyril was banished from the house during daylight hours.

He knew all too well that needs could technically be met and yet a child could be so much in want. In want of affection. In want of joy. In want of peace and security. In want of the freedom to be who God had made them. He hadn't known any of those things until his father died. Mariah did—and he wasn't going to sit here and let anyone take them from her.

Cyril forked a vegetable and grinned. "Ri, do you remember the time we had asparagus when we were children? We were eating in the nursery, and your governess had gone to fetch something. I believe I started it by observing that this would make a most becoming sword for a small warrior."

There. The corners of Mariah's mouth turned up. "I thought Miss Featherstone would never let us eat together again when she found us sword-fighting with them."

75

Cyril laughed, as did Castleton from the head of the table, though the others scowled. "I say," the earl began, "I don't believe I heard about this. Though I can't imagine Miss Featherstone being that angry if you were simply dueling at your seats." His eyes gleamed as he waited for the rest of the story.

Mariah's blush made her cheeks glow. "One can't properly fence when seated, Papa. We had no choice but to take the battle all over the nursery."

The memory played out in Cyril's mind like a play on a stage. "I would have won, had Mariah not gained the higher ground. She stabbed me through just as the governess reentered."

Castleton lifted his brows. "And that higher ground was . . . ?"

Mariah tried and failed to stifle her laughter. "The table, naturally."

"Oh, Mariah." Lady Castleton pressed a hand to her head, as if the long-past indiscretion physically pained her.

Her husband waved it off. "Lighten up, darling. She was only a child. It was ages ago—and obviously Miss Featherstone took her in hand if she didn't even feel the need to come to us about it." He winked at his youngest stepchild. "Isn't that right, sweetling?"

"We were well and thoroughly punished," Mariah agreed with a decisive nod. And a quick, amused glance at Cyril.

He grinned back. The governess had indeed tried to punish them by making them clean the nursery from top to bottom the next day rather than go outside. But they'd turned that into a game too and had so much fun that Featherstone had declared it hopeless and had collapsed onto her favorite sofa, laughing. She'd called them both over to her side and had made them tell her the story they'd been acting out—and had then encouraged them to write it down.

It was how they'd ended up with that document Mariah had brought out and shown him. They'd taken turns, paragraph by paragraph, telling the tale they'd devised. They'd decided the adventure should begin inside, rather than out—in the formal parlor, where the enormous Christmas tree resided. The nutcracker doll had been cast as the hero, a little girl rather like Mariah as the heroine, and a ghastly mouse, enemy to the toys, as the villain. Because it kept sneaking in and stealing Mariah's favorite candies, threatening to chew her favorite dolls to bits if she didn't hand them over.

Naturally, the valiant nutcracker had fought him off, but the story didn't end there. Though the mouse king retreated, he didn't declare a truce. He merely bided his time until he'd gathered more of his troops and lured them out into the wood. The nutcracker and Mariah rallied the dolls and toys and led them to a glorious victory, which they celebrated by touring the nutcracker's fairy kingdom—through the Almond Gate, into Christmas Wood, over Orange Creek, and down to Orgeat Lake.

How Cyril wished he'd been here last week to see how the village children brought the tale to life in their little play. Had he known it was happening, he would have made it a point to arrive earlier.

Even without hearing the rest of the tale, the earl continued to chuckle. "Ah, I'd forgot how well the two of you got along. Lord Gyldenkrone, you'll find that our dear Mariah can brighten any room with her imagination, even now—and she brings delight to those in her care. She is absolutely adored by our neighbors, especially the children."

"Very true." Lady Castleton brightened, leaning forward after the servants cleared the plates from before her. "She will make the most beloved mistress of whatever home she ends up calling her own. Her compassionate heart is beyond compare."

Beside him, Louise sighed and leaned back to allow her own plate to be removed as well. "It's very true. She is still plying the poor with candies and fairy tales when we're not on hand to advise bread instead. She delivers the hats and scarves Mother and I knit too."

Gyldenkrone inclined his head, either impressed or wanting to look it. "And does Lady Mariah knit for the less fortunate as well?"

Louise's small smile looked apologetic. "We did try to teach her, but Mariah never much cared for yarn arts. Did you, dearest?"

Cyril didn't like Louise much better now than he had at age ten.

Mariah, however, smiled. "I was an utter dunce at both knitting and crochet. But I like to think that I still contribute. It is important to tend their bodies, yes. But just as important to tend their souls."

Gyldenkrone's surprise was clearly false. "Have you no vicar nearby to do that?"

Mariah's chin lifted a notch. "Of course we have. And he is a wonderful man. But Jesus never said that the rest of us were released from the duty just because there is a clergyman nearby. We are all called to minister to those in need—"

"With food and clothing and medicine," Louise put in calmly.

"And is laughter not the best medicine? Can joy and hope not accomplish what science fails to achieve?"

Castleton was poised to intervene, but a loud gong sounded at that moment, bringing instant silence to the table. The family knew what the noise was about—Lord and Lady Castleton and Mariah's eyes lit with happy expectation, and Louise and Fred exchanged a resigned glance, Louise muttering something about the pudding having to wait, as it always did on this day.

Cyril found his own gaze wandering to the only other stranger, and Gyldenkrone looked at him too. No doubt Cyril's confusion showed on his face just as the Dane's did.

The gong sounded again, and the Castletons pushed back from the table, both smiling and motioning with their hands. "Come, come," the lady all but sang.

"The professor is ready," his lordship added, presumably for Cyril's and Gyldenkrone's benefit.

Mariah was on her feet in a flash, Cyril matching her, the others moving more slowly. Since everyone seemed to be darting or trudging from the table at their own pace, he ignored his assigned dinner companion in favor of catching Mariah up at the door.

"What's going on?" he asked in a whisper. "Is this what he mentioned unveiling this evening?"

Mariah nodded so enthusiastically that a lock of hair escaped its pins and fluttered down to frame her face. "He always creates a masterpiece—part sculpture, part clockworks, part toy—to display for the Christmas Eve Ball. Something new every year, and then he takes it apart again in the new year and reuses the bits and gears for the next one. The children love it!"

She did too, clearly. Cyril made no attempt to restrain his grin. "But it was obviously in pieces in his workshop—could he have put it together already?"

Mariah shook her head and followed her parents toward the ballroom. "There will be details yet unfinished, but he always lets us see it as soon as he has the shell assembled, so that we can help with some of the positioning of figures on their tracks." Her laugh rang like music through the corridor. "Because I think he knows I would sneak in and reposition them otherwise."

He could well imagine it. "How long has the professor been in residence?"

"This will be his tenth year with us," the earl answered from ahead of them, turning to smile at Cyril. "He was my tutor as a child, then went on to teach at Cambridge. When he retired, I begged him to make Plumford Manor his home, and after a visit in which I promised to convert that old outbuilding into a workshop for him, he agreed. I knew his goal was to spend his later years tinkering on toys. But even I underestimated the delight he would bring to the neighborhood." He paused, considering. "He has a pension from the university, but I've granted him his own living space and the workshop here, and a small stipend besides, for the service he gave me in my youth. It is our joint wish that he'll be able to live out his days here."

Those days would likely expire long before the earl's did—the professor had to be in his mid-eighties—but nonetheless, Cyril knew well what Castleton was getting at. He wanted assurances that if by some ill-fate he left this earth before the professor, the old man wouldn't be kicked to the curb.

Cyril could grant that most happily with a nod every bit as enthusiastic as Mariah's had been. "Of course! I've only spent an hour in his company, but it was sheer wonder. I'm greatly looking forward to becoming better acquainted with him. I have no doubt we would have endless things to talk about—literature and science and his new work besides."

They came to a halt at the closed French doors of the ballroom, their windowed panes covered from within by some dark fabric that hadn't been there earlier when he'd walked by. Castleton watched behind them, nodding his approval once the shuffling steps of the dawdlers said they'd finally caught up. Cyril resisted the urge to peek back at their faces. Their slow steps had told him everything he needed to know about their opinions of the professor's creations. Better to focus on the happiness of his other three companions.

Once assembled, Castleton knocked on the door and called out, "We're here, Professor!"

"Enter!"

The earl swung the doors wide and led the way into the dark room. Even with some light creeping in from the corridor, it was difficult to make out anything other than the large, open expanse and a few hulking shapes that were probably chairs, sideboards, and perhaps a grand piano there in the corner.

Mariah must have shifted closer to him as they moved cautiously inside. Her arm pressed against his, not retreating again as quickly as he might have expected, which suited him fine. He caught the scent of whatever she used on her hair—something fruity rather than floral—mixed with the unmistakable fragrance of cinnamon and spice.

Someone must have sneaked off to the kitchen again before

dinner to help with the holiday baking. He grinned into the dark. Perhaps if he asked nicely, she'd take him with her next time.

Without warning, the lights blazed to life, electricity setting the chandeliers to twinkling, a million shattered rainbows dancing through the crystal drops and onto the parquet dance floor. Cyril blinked his eyes back into focus, his gaze traveling the room.

A Christmas tree loomed in the center of the back wall, framed by the ballroom's massive floor-to-ceiling windows. It was yet undecorated, but its towering height and wide arms promised dazzling beauty in a few days. Greenery draped every window, as well as the massive fireplace at the end opposite the tree.

The professor, however, was scurrying away from the light switch and toward one of the far corners, where something large was swathed in concealing fabric. It was shorter than the tree by half but taller than the man by at least a foot, wide and deep and with many protrusions poking at the cloth.

Mariah gripped his arm, no doubt more from anticipation than affection. He'd take it, though, and hope that Gyldenkrone saw it too. A check to the man's confidence would do him good.

All right, so Gyldenkrone's good wasn't really Cyril's motivation. He mostly hoped the man would squirm. He didn't honestly know him that well, and until last week he would have called him distant and cool but upright and of sound character. Now, though? A man of sound character didn't let his brother defame a lady.

Cyril straightened his spine, new determination settling on him. He'd defended Pearl's reputation from Emil Gyldenkrone's claims—and she'd thanked him for it by cutting him to ribbons and declaring she intended to marry the greve.

Yet here was the greve, inexplicably pursuing Mariah instead of Pearl.

A better choice, yes. He could see that quite clearly after merely a day and a half in Mariah's company. She was all things sweet and lovely and charming.

And she deserved far better than a cold, unfeeling nobleman interested only in her connections and put off by her personality. If he wouldn't defend Pearl against his brother's claims, he wouldn't defend Mariah against Louise's sour behavior or the world's insistence that she give up her whimsy in favor of practicality. And in the Danish court? Would he defend his bride if his king or prince or princess said a word against her?

Hardly.

If the greve convinced the Lightbournes and Lyons, convinced Mariah herself, to make a match, Cyril had a sinking feeling that his old friend would end up miserable. Stifled by the Dane's ice, by the court's expectations. That precious, flickering light of joy he saw inside her snuffed out by worries and concerns and the sure knowledge that she could never please the ones who ought to love her best.

No. No, he couldn't let that future befall her. He knew too well what it was to want desperately to be loved and instead be dismissed or relegated to the sidelines. To be expected to fit a mold and, if you failed, to be sneered and slapped at.

Mariah would *not* find in marriage what his mother had. Her children would *not* be treated as mere possessions, as he had been.

He was none too certain, honestly, that Emil hadn't been speaking truth about his conquest of Pearl, however ungenteel it had been to brag about it. Cyril had defended *her* simply because it had been the gentlemanly thing to do.

But Mariah—Mariah was deserving of all happiness, all good things. She deserved to be championed. She deserved a true hero. She deserved a story that was more than political arrangements and distance.

The professor cleared his throat, calling attention back to himself, and then without any further ado, whipped the cloth cover from his creation. A castle emerged that made them gasp—even stoic Gyldenkrone and sour Louise and grumpy Fred.

Cyril wasn't even aware of moving, only of needing a closer look. The rest of the company agreed, because in the next moment they were fanned out about it, examining each working door and window, following with eyes and fingers the small metal tracks that went hither and yon, promising mechanical life once the professor had positioned the occupants. Its spires and turrets stretched upward with unbelievable grace, shaded in blues and whites and purples.

Gyldenkrone stood back a step, but appreciation colored his face. "It is Neuschwanstein Castle, is it not?"

"More or less, yes." The professor smiled, pleased by the reactions. "I took a few liberties here and there, but it was my inspiration, without question."

"I have spent quite a bit of time exploring that castle," the greve said. "It is a remarkable likeness. You are very talented, Professor."

"It's breathtaking." Mariah indeed sounded as though she couldn't drag enough air into her lungs, her eyes wide with awe. "I can't imagine the real thing being any better."

Smooth as silk, Gyldenkrone moved to her side—but his gaze moved to Cyril. "Perhaps I'll take you there someday, Lady Mariah. And you can judge the two, though you will only be more impressed by the professor's attention to detail, not less."

Cyril folded his arms across his chest. He saw it for what it was—a gauntlet tossed down. He just wasn't certain exactly how to pick it up but to prove himself the older friend, the chosen companion, the one who would call home this place she loved so much. "Where are the figures, Professor? You already had Mariah choose the roles of a few, didn't you?"

And the glint in the greve's eyes said he too recognized a challenge when he heard it.

A new game, it seemed, was on. A race to win Lady Mariah.

But Cyril couldn't help but think he had the edge. Gyldenkrone might be seeking her hand—but he wasn't seeking her heart. And that, Cyril knew, was the true prize.

If only he knew how to convince her that he could be more than the friend adventuring at her side. He could be the hero seeking only to bring her joy. What would it take to make her see that, though?

8

With only four days left until Christmas—and only three until the ball—Mariah wasn't the only one in Castleton with a spring in her step as she exited the prettily arched stone doorway of St. Edmund's church on Sunday morning. Everywhere she looked were smiling faces, excited promises to see her soon, and excited chatter over the play of the week before. At least, at first. Then she caught the looks of disappointment the villagers sent her parents, when they talked of the play that their lord and lady had missed.

Mariah kept her smile in place as she made her way back to the family carriages, pushing down the sorrow at those long looks. Papa and Mama had always made a point of being part of the community, of supporting and encouraging them. But that only made it more disappointing when they didn't show up for something. It was a small rift, a trifling slight . . . but still a rift, still a slight, and she hated to see it. Hated to realize that something had already tarnished the Christmas season for her neighbors. Hated the discomfort Papa fought as he tried to assure them that he'd not miss the next children's play.

She sighed. It was a small thing. It would soon be forgotten. And even as she longed to somehow set it to rights, she knew that

Christmas at Sugar Plum Manor

it was silly of her. She would focus instead on bringing new cheer, wherever she could. Reminding everyone of what joy still waited this Christmas.

Nearing the two carriages they'd had to bring to fit them all, she waited to see which one Louise entered before choosing the second instead.

Granted, if anyone needed some holiday cheer, it was Louise. But her sister stoutly refused to feel it, and there was only so much a girl could do. To put a new spin on an old adage, one could lead a widow to a party, but one couldn't make her dance.

Perhaps Lord Gyldenkrone had been hanging back with similar calculation, because he climbed in right behind Mariah. Mama and Cyril followed, leaving Papa and Fred to join Louise. Not that the greve seemed to mind her sister's company or conversation, but he was nothing if not resolute. She had to give him that. He'd declared his intention to pursue Mariah, and he'd been at her side every moment he could manage it since he arrived.

His nearness made her chest go tight. It was flattering. And the prospect of so handsome a man seeking her hand and then whisking her away to another kingdom, into the very court of its royalty . . . it was fit for any of the fairy tales she'd devoured as a girl.

And yet she couldn't help but feel like she didn't measure up to his expectations—or at least his desires. He'd made it so clear that her view of the world was something to be tolerated and corrected, not indulged or embraced.

Maybe he was right. Maybe it was time to put aside the last vestiges of those "childish things." Maybe it was time to admit that while a girl could dream of toys coming to life and princes sweeping her away, a woman must focus on needful things. Bread instead of candy. Scarves instead of stories.

Maybe it was time to be more like Louise. Less like . . . herself.

Heaviness settled on her shoulders.

Mama made small talk with Gyldenkrone about the differences between their own church services and the Lutheran ones he was accustomed to attending in Copenhagen, but his answers were brief. Too brief, apparently, because after giving them, he turned his face to Mariah, where she sat beside her mother, his focus sharp and unswerving.

"My lady," he said in that crisp voice of his, "I was hoping you would join me on a promenade after we've got back to the house. Before luncheon."

He didn't, she noticed, phrase it as a question. Her throat went dry. "Oh. Ah . . ."

"She would be delighted." Mama reached over, twining their gloved fingers together and giving Mariah's a squeeze that felt more like warning than support.

"Delighted," Mariah mumbled, praying her smile looked more confident than it felt on her lips.

Soon they were pulling round the circle at the top of the drive— and Mama was resolutely gripping her arm. "Mariah will be down directly," she said to the greve, her smile sugary and her eyes like steel. "After she changes into more suitable clothes for the outing, my lord."

"I shall await her most eagerly."

Mariah didn't know exactly why her mother had gone so determined, but she didn't even attempt to exchange a fortifying glance with Cyril. Given his feelings for the greve, he likely wouldn't have any encouragement to silently send her way. No, she would have to find the strength to face his intimidating façade within herself.

Her mother waited only until Mariah's bedroom door had closed behind them before turning on her with drawn brows and a low, chiding voice. "What is wrong with you, dearest? You act as though his attention is unwelcome."

"Not unwelcome. Just . . . terrifying." Mariah sank onto the side of her mattress while Mama bustled over to her armoire and pulled out a warm woolen walking dress. "Have you not noticed how he dislikes me?"

"Nonsense." Mama tossed the green dress onto her bed and

sat beside her. "He made his intentions quite clear to your papa. Why would he do that if he disliked you?"

"Because of Papa! Because of Fred. Not because of me." Her head sank down toward her chest, and she felt an even heavier burden when Mama's arm slipped around her back.

"Sweetling, you don't know your own charms. He is infatuated."

A snort slipped out. "And you accuse *me* of an overactive imagination."

She oughtn't to have said it. Even without looking up, she could hear her mother's accusatory breath, feel it in her arm. "Mariah. He is a fine man, and he would not have stated his intention if he didn't mean it."

"I have no doubt he meant it. It's only . . ." She drew in a long breath, focusing her gaze on the wall opposite her instead of her mother. "He is here because of *what* I am, not because of *who* I am. It wouldn't matter what I was like, so long as I'm Fred's sister and Papa's stepdaughter. He'd still be just as interested."

"Nonsense," Mama said again. "If one's circumstances were all he cared about, he would have proposed to Lady Pearl already."

Was that supposed to help? Mariah picked up the wool dress but just held it in her lap. "No doubt he would have, had she not made it clear she preferred Cyril. My working theory, anyway."

"Is that what this is about? Jealousy of Pearl Kingeland?"

Was it? Perhaps, in a way. But more, it was disappointment that no man seemed to see through Pearl's beautiful face. Was that the same thing as jealousy? Just as petty?

She took another deep breath and stood. "Perhaps it is. Perhaps I need to move past that. Or ask him outright what he feels for her." Though even if he claimed not to have had a stitch of affection for Pearl, that didn't mean he had any more for Mariah. Her shoulders sagged again. "Is it so big an ask, that my future husband would prefer me to others? For who I am?"

Mama stood too and turned Mariah gently around so she could work on the buttons up her back. "My sweet girl. Whoever you end up marrying will love you beyond measure. How could they not?"

Or what if they only would if she changed? If she put aside the things Louise called ridiculous, if she stopped saying the things that made Lord Gyldenkrone frown? What if that was what it would take to make him like her?

Was it worth it?

"I will not tell you that you must marry him," Mama said, having reached the end of the buttons but holding Mariah in place with hands on her shoulders. "That is up to you. But hear him out. Give it due consideration. Pause to think about what it would mean, dearest. Not just the life he could give you, but the promise for your children. One of them could be a prince or princess—think about that. Your child or grandchild could sit on one of Europe's thrones. Does that not appeal to your romantic notions? Does it not ignite those dreams you dream so well?"

It certainly had appeal . . . but what did crowns and wealth and connections matter if you didn't have love?

But Mama would only point out that her first marriage had been made for the usual reasons, as had Louise's, but that both had turned out well enough. She'd remind her that love had come with Mariah's father, as it had between Louise and Swann. And then Mariah would get that odd little squiggle in her chest that always pounced whenever her mother talked of the father she didn't even remember, of arrangements and alliances and the blessing that followed when one did the right thing instead of the selfish thing.

Was she selfish? She let herself be prodded toward the dressing screen and changed mechanically from her church dress into the walking dress.

"There now." Mama clapped her hands to Mariah's wool-clad arms when she emerged again and beamed. "You look beautiful. Lord Gyldenkrone cannot help but be enchanted by you, sweetling. So let's go down there, and you take that walk with him—and you will give him a fair chance. Do you understand me?"

Mariah nodded. She knew her parents had only her good in mind. And she knew that the greve was as fine a man as Mama said. She couldn't deny the allure of all he stood for, all he offered . . . but still her hands shook with nerves.

Maybe . . . surely . . . if she got to know Gyldenkrone, if he got to know her, then . . . something. Something would change. Either she'd realize he wasn't so cold and unfeeling, that he *did* have warm feelings for her buried under that perfect veneer of ice, or he would realize that her whimsy was part of who she was. Or both. They could meet somewhere in the middle, perhaps.

Somehow as she lectured herself thus, Mama had propelled her out of her room and down the stairs and directly to the greve. He smiled and held out an arm, and really, what cause did she have to think both gestures were only playacting? She ought to focus on the positive.

He was handsome—very handsome. Well-chiseled features, that arctic blond hair, and the arm she rested her hand on was solid, muscled. His figure hinted at more of the same beneath his well-tailored clothes.

Solid and muscled like a wolf.

Silliness. She fought it off with a smile as he led her outside and toward the garden path.

The air was cold but the wind calm today, and the bite in the air made her turn her face toward the sky. No clouds—not yet. But she had a hope that they would come before Christmas and give them a new blanket of snow. The world always looked so beautiful when it was covered with a few inches of fluffy white.

She turned to her companion, figuring that was always a safe topic of conversation. "You get more snow in Denmark than we do here, isn't that right?"

He glanced down at her, no expression on his face to give her a clue as to his thoughts. "Quite. We average over a hundred and fifty inches of snow a year, usually coming in storms that leave half a foot at a time. Do you like the snow?"

"I love it." The dusting they'd gotten last Wednesday still clung here and there in the garden, though it had lost its initial luster. "As long as it lets up. I do like being able to get out."

"Then you will love Denmark." *Will*, he said, not *would*. "We are not too cold, not like some of the other Scandinavian countries. Our winter temperatures usually hover just around the freezing point."

There, see? Weather was a perfectly pleasant topic of conversation between them. She was about to ask him what the summers were like, but he spoke again before she could.

"I trust your parents have relayed to you my intentions?"

Her mouth went as parched as a desert. Or perhaps the tundra, given the chill. "They . . . hinted."

"Well, allow me to remove any need for speculation." He paused, turning to face her. The safety of the house directly behind her, the promise of freedom in the wood beyond him. He took both her hands in his, and though two layers of gloves separated their skin, she would have sworn she felt an extra chill seeping through. "It is my goal to take you with me back to Copenhagen in the new year as my bride-to-be."

Take her . . . as his . . .

The world swam. Mariah had to blink it back into focus, but his determined, emotionless face still hovered there before her. Yes, she'd known his intentions were serious, but . . . she'd expected him to ask for permission to court her, not inform her then and there that she was the one he'd chosen. That he meant to take her away not in a half year but *now*. In two short weeks.

"I don't understand." Her words came out halting, uncertain. "Why? Why would you set your sights on me?"

His scowl was a bit of an improvement over his usual impassive mask—at least it showed a bit of emotion. "Your family is beyond compare, which you must know. The list of appropriate ladies is short, and I have decided you best suit my needs."

"Suit your needs?" Now her voice was faint enough to be embarrassing.

"And I can offer you what no one else can, connections beyond your wildest dreams. Which is saying something, is it not? If you want to dine with princesses and live in fairy-tale castles, I can give you that. We can travel the world, meet the royalty of Europe—or if benevolence is your preference, I would grant a generous stipend for such worthy work."

She had to shake her head a bit to dislodge his pretty words. Pretty, but horribly incomplete. "What about love? Or at least affection?"

"Love?" He didn't exactly scoff—but he didn't exactly not. "The romantic sort you likely have in mind is too flimsy a foundation for something as serious as marriage. Marriage ought to be founded on respect, trust, and mutual benefit."

She tugged her fingers free of his. "And do you have that for me? Respect? Trust?"

"Of course." He had the decency, at least, to pause after the quick response. Tilt his head. "Or at least I'm certain I shall. Once we know each other better."

"So then instead of declaring your intention of marrying me here and now, perhaps we ought to do that—get to know each other better." She lifted her chin. "You'd granted that much to Lady Pearl, hadn't you?"

Cool amusement glinted in his eyes. "I did—and found her lacking. But it was caution on my part that made me tread slowly with her, given that I saw her nature in an instant. I do not see the same cause for alarm in you, my lady. And I am afraid my time is running short. I have business I must attend to in Denmark, and I would like to have my fiancée with me when I go, so that introductions can be made."

In one second she was mollified that at least *he* had seen through Pearl, even if Cyril hadn't. In the next, trepidation struck anew. "But . . . that is so soon. I realize society matches are often made quickly, but, honestly, my lord, until two days ago, I didn't think you'd given me more than a passing thought, for me to have considered *you* in any seriousness. And what you offer represents a monumental change for me. I cannot make a decision so hastily. I need time to consider, and to get to know you. To be assured that love could, at least, come in time."

His glower slammed back into place. "I am already thirty-one years old, my lady, and my prince is wed and having children. I have no more time to waste on placating feminine dreams of romance. I need a wife, and I need one now. Your stepfather has already agreed to the match if you consent, as has your brother. The only thing lacking is your agreement."

Her heart thudded, but it wasn't with excitement. Was this really her first proposal? Not a question, but a statement of fact? One in which he not only made no promises of love but deemed the expectation ridiculous?

Her eyes felt disastrously hot, but she blinked back any impending tears before they could disgrace her and lifted her chin. "I grant that you haven't years more to waste. But a few days to let me consider your offer is certainly not asking too much."

His face smoothed again, the icy mask unmelted by the smile he pasted onto his lips. "A few days' consideration is perfectly reasonable. This is a big decision, you're right, but I know that when you take the time to think about it, you will see the wisdom in accepting my proposal. I will be a good husband to you, Lady Mariah. Never will you have to doubt my fidelity or loyalty. You will never want for a thing. You will have a friend eager to welcome you to her side in Princess Alexandrine. She will usher you immediately into her inner court, guaranteeing other friends who will look up to you and admire you."

Perhaps the thought of instant popularity would have made Pearl or even Louise preen, but it made her shrink away another step. Lovely as it sounded on paper, the truth was that she didn't want a royal court in some foreign land—or even her own. She didn't want fawning flatterers or state-sanctioned friendships or a marriage built on nothing but political maneuvering.

She wanted home. She wanted family. She wanted the security of knowing that she was loved for who she was. "You don't even like me. You think me ridiculous." As she said the words, she wasn't sure if they were an argument or a plea for him to reassure her.

His release of breath wasn't quite a sigh. But it wasn't quite not either. "Silly, perhaps. But you are very young—it's to be expected. I don't hold it against you."

Blessed heat burned her cheeks. "I rather hope I never lose the ability to focus on joy, nor the desire to bring it to others. And I rather hope to be appreciated *for* it and not despite it." She forced her lips up a few degrees. "But perhaps that *is* silly."

He sighed. "I mean no insult, my lady. Please, be assured that I have considered all the young ladies I have met since my arrival with the utmost care, and you have proven yourself the best possible candidate. Much as the Kingeland family had its advantages, Lady Pearl would have ruined them with her dishonest, faithless ways. You, on the other hand, I could tell within a single exchange . . . are completely innocuous."

Perhaps he meant it as a compliment, but it needled like an insult, pulling sarcasm to her lips before she could bite it back. "Innocuous. Oh please, my lord, stop with these sweet nothings. You'll turn my head."

He narrowed his eyes. "I hope it's to my credit that I'm not trying to. I'm presenting no flattery or lies to win your favor. Only simple facts."

She folded her arms over her chest, though it did little to make her warmer—not given that the cold came from within even more than without. She didn't want flattery or lies, but a bit of trying to win her favor wouldn't go awry. Wasn't there a way to do that and be truthful?

Apparently not. Her shoulders sagged. Maybe Louise and Fred and Mama were right. Maybe it was time to put aside the Mariah she had always been. Maybe to refuse would be to deny herself any future worth having. And even Papa thought Gyldenkrone a good match for her. He'd agreed to the greve's request for a blessing, hadn't he? And Papa was an excellent judge of character.

"There. I see you're genuinely considering it." Gyldenkrone reached out, hesitated a moment, and then touched a hand lightly to her elbow. "Do so for the next few days. Let us say that you shall give me your answer on Christmas Eve, hmm? It will be a most felicitous thing to announce at your family's ball."

He didn't lack for confidence, clearly. It didn't even occur to him that she would say no.

She nodded, hoping the emotions churning inside her— emotions he didn't fall prey to—wouldn't come weeping out here and now.

"Good." He smiled another cold, joyless smile and gave her elbow a little squeeze. "I will await your answer."

He strode away, back toward the house, leaving her alone in the winter garden with her bleak choices and cold fingers. He could have at least asked properly—couldn't he have? He could have found something to praise other than her family and the fact that she was innocuous.

"Innocuous." The word boiled up out of her, warming her enough to stir her into action. Ignoring the house and its promise of fire and food, she stalked out of the gardens, past the professor's workshop, and into the wood.

The entrance she'd chosen wasn't near the two curving branches that she and Cyril had dubbed Almond Gate, but the same creek ran along this side of the property. She found a rock at its edge, brushed the last remains of snow from its top, and sank to a chilly seat on its hard surface.

Tears stung her eyes anew, and this time she let them come.

This wasn't what she'd imagined her first marriage proposal would be like—but was she a goose for being hung up on that? Who ever received the proposal of their dreams, anyway? And really, she didn't need the magic of drifting snow crystals floating around her or the man to drop to one knee. She didn't need a sparkling gemstone displayed then and there in his hands, or pretty words full of pledges of eternal, undying love.

She just needed to know that the man to whom she would promise her life would cherish her and at least come to love her.

The tears were hot on her cold cheeks. She couldn't honestly imagine Lord Gyldenkrone giving her that sort of proposal. Could he come to care? He *could*. No matter how cool the exterior, she had to think him capable of love, certainly of devotion. If she had the leisure to get to know him, to learn those depths, perhaps it would be different. At the moment, though, it felt as though their desires were more at cross-purposes.

She wanted someone to love her for who she was. He wanted someone to trust him that the future would be everything he promised.

But if she were being completely honest, part of the reason she couldn't imagine Gyldenkrone giving her that sort of proposal was because in her old imaginings, another man had always been the one down on his knee, snow swirling about him. She hadn't known what he would look like, all grown up. She hadn't known if he'd have turned into the man she'd hoped he would. She'd just known that, until Mama forced their letters to be so horribly proper, Cyril Lightbourne had been the only one in the world who truly seemed to know her. To understand her. And to like her anyway.

And yet Cyril Lightbourne *wasn't* the man she'd hoped he'd become. He was exactly the sort she feared they all were—too taken in by a pretty face and melodic voice to spare a glance to what lay beneath. Too quick to become one of Lady Pearl's minions.

It made so little sense, now that he was back and they'd picked up where they left off. He didn't *seem* like he should be that sort. He still spoke of ideals and ideas, of novels and poetry, of sermons and histories. He was *not* shallow.

And yet it was Gyldenkrone who had seen through Pearl. Cyril who was still her devoted servant.

Mariah stared at the water trickling beneath the layer of ice, pushing its way up here and there and then tumbling down again. The longer she watched, the more it spoke of a truth far deeper than water and ice. The more it reminded her that these people around her were just the same. They only ever got glimpses of each other's hearts, then they buried their feelings again under responsibilities and expectations, duties and obligations.

Cyril, who had let himself remain a mystery to protect his insecure heart, too wounded by his own father to trust the goodness of hers.

Lord Gyldenkrone, who didn't dare to show his deepest heart to a collection of strangers not even from his country, who all waited to judge him for any misstep.

Mama, who worked so tirelessly for her children's happiness that she too often forgot to take a moment and just be there in her own happily-ever-after.

Papa, who too often gave up trying to be the father her siblings needed for fear of being rebuffed again.

Fred, who had let the responsibilities of their father's estate rob him of the joy of childhood and turn him into a terse, bitter man.

Louise, who had suffered such grief that she didn't dare hope for brighter days.

She stared at the water, imagining that as she traced its course, she could trace the riverbeds of love and loss, hope and despair, that had carved each of them into the people they were. She imagined life as the water that cut its path through them.

And yet that water went only where the Lord directed it. He sent it from the heavens. He poured it into the oceans. He carved those rivers and streams with the tip of His finger.

That same finger had carved her into who she was, able to receive that same life. To let it flow or to stop it off.

As the sun shone on the ice, a new piece of it cracked, melted, and slipped away with that fast-flowing water fighting to be seen again.

Resolved, Mariah pushed from her seat, cast her eyes around the familiar scene of Christmas Wood, and smiled.

Perhaps life always left them covered in ice—but it didn't have to stay that way. Sometimes one had to push through the hard things. Sometimes one had to bubble in joy. Sometimes one had to shift so that the sun could shine down, even on the coldest days.

Sometimes that bleak winter just needed the light of Christmas. And maybe, if she could remind them of that . . . maybe, if she could help shine that light . . . maybe, if she could show them that joy was more than whimsy, that it was a gift from God sent to earth for each of them . . . well, then maybe this Christmas could be more than awkward guests and disappointing proposals. Maybe, just maybe, it could be a Christmas they'd remember as the one where they'd reclaimed that magic they hadn't felt since childhood.

And maybe, if she helped them see it as she did . . . maybe they'd stop trying to tell her she was looking at it wrong. Maybe, just maybe, they'd grant that one could be a reasonable adult and still see the world with imaginative eyes and with a heart ready to believe.

9

Cyril pulled his cape coat on, jammed his hat onto his head, and dashed out into the wintry air. His gaze latched onto the spot of red all but skipping toward Almond Gate. He considered calling out, but it was still awfully early—the sun had scarcely stretched its fingers over the horizon, and no one else in the family had put in an appearance for breakfast yet. So instead of a shout, he opted for a lope, closing the distance between them with gratifying quickness.

When Mariah hadn't joined the family for the meal the night before, Cyril had been more than a little concerned. He'd wanted to catch her after her walk with the greve yesterday, but she had gone off into the wood instead of coming back inside, and Castleton had intercepted him when he thought to go after her. The earl had said he merely wanted to share a game of chess to continue their growing friendship, but he suspected it was more that he hadn't wanted Cyril inserting himself into his stepdaughter's musings after whatever Gyldenkrone had said to her.

By the time he'd pried himself free of the game and conversation—which had been pleasant enough, aside from the obvious motivations behind it—he'd caught just a glimpse of Mariah disappearing into her room. Where she had stayed, blast her, until now. And "family" or not, he couldn't just go knocking on her bedroom door. If he tried that one, he'd no doubt find himself dismissed to the bachelor wing in half a heartbeat. So he'd resorted to spending his hours with a book, though he could scarcely recall what he'd read.

The morning light was cool and blue, each flat surface etched with a lace of frost that made him pause for just a moment and catch his breath in awe. The Lord's artistry always amazed him. All the more so when he considered the different brushes and strokes and color palettes He used. Reds and golds in the autumn, greens and yellows in the spring, deeper variations in the summer. And then this—a muted world of silver and blue and purple, glassed over with frost and ice and snow.

"Mariah!" Once in the little forest that would capture his shout and keep it from echoing back to the manor house, he dared to call out. "Wait up."

She hadn't been in sight, but she quickly appeared in it again, on the path they'd already taken several times since he'd arrived. Her face gave him pause again. She looked . . . odd. A bit resigned. A bit hopeful. A bit as though she were somewhere far, far away, and no amount of running would catch him up to her.

Fear speared his chest. What if it was Denmark that had her dreaming? Gyldenkrone? What if she'd already made up her mind to bind her life to that of the coldhearted wolf of a greve?

No. She was right there, moving closer every second, and even with a smile on her lips. He hadn't lost her yet. "You're out and about early this morning, Cyril."

He made certain his grin was as warm as it ought to be. "I might say the same to you. Though I, at least, had the wherewithal to visit the kitchen first." He reached his hand into his pocket and pulled out the napkins that held two squares of gingerbread, still warm. He held one out to her. "With Mrs. Trutchen's 'good morning.'"

Her smile went warmer as she reached for the cake. "Ah, heavenly. My thanks to both of you."

He waited a moment, but she didn't invite him to join her, just took a long, appreciative sniff of the spiced, fluffy treat and then broke off a piece and popped it into her mouth. Well. He wasn't going to let a little thing like that deter him. "Mind if I walk with you? I could use the exercise."

"Oh." He tried not to take it as an insult when uncertainty and anxiety flashed across her face. "I . . . I wasn't really walking. I was going to sit and do some writing."

He hadn't at first noticed the little satchel she had slung over her shoulder, but it must contain a notebook and pen. "Oh." He felt his shoulders slump a bit. "I don't want to interrupt. Though if you wouldn't mind a bit of company at least while you eat?"

A smile claimed her lips, small but genuine. "I wouldn't mind at all. I thought to settle at Giant's Table anyway."

He grinned back. "Perfect." The path wasn't wide enough for them to walk two abreast in this part of the wood, but it opened up just before the ancient slabs of rock that had, to his ten-year-old mind, once been the feasting table and benches for a family of giants.

Mariah scrambled up with ease that proved she did it often, slinging her bag onto the table-rock and setting her gingerbread beside it. "I don't suppose Mrs. Trutchen sent out any tea along with the cake? Or milk?"

He chuckled and sat on the bench-stone beside her. "I'm afraid not. Sorry." He took a bite of his own warm treat, savoring the rich explosion of spices on his tongue. Molasses, ginger, cinnamon—Christmas in a single bite. He stole a glance at her. "Are you feeling well? We missed you last night."

I missed you last night—that was what he meant to say. But couching it in a plural seemed safer.

She kept her face turned toward her breakfast. "Quite well." No excuse followed, not even the trite claim of a headache.

Obviously a more straightforward tactic was required. He angled himself to face her. "All right then, out with it. What did he say to you? On that walk yesterday?"

She shrugged. Which didn't match the words she followed it with. "Just that he wanted to marry me."

Cyril nearly choked on the bite of gingerbread he'd been chewing and had to cough a few times to clear his airway before he dared to look at her again. "What? He proposed?"

Another of those lying shrugs. "Not exactly. He more . . . informed me of his intentions and requested my decision by the ball."

Cyril slapped a gloved hand to the cold rock. "Well why didn't you give it to him then and there? It's absurd. You can't marry him."

"Can't?" Now she lifted her delicate brows, a hint of life sparking in her eyes.

He probably had no right, as the far-removed cousin of her stepfather, to forbid it. But oh, how he wanted to. "You barely know him!"

"I know him as well as Louise knew Lord Swann."

"He's wrong for you."

She studied her food again, picking it apart rather than eating it. "How can I know that? Mama and Papa like him well enough—they approve of the match."

And why was she arguing for this? "He's an utter cad."

"What?" That got her attention, and she sent a hard frown his way. "I've heard no such rumors about his character, and he was quite direct about the importance of uprightness."

"He just stood by and let his brother brag about luring Lady Pearl into a heated embrace!" He had the sinking feeling, as he watched a veritable parade of emotions flit across her face too rapidly for him to keep up with, that it was the wrong thing to say.

She swallowed a small, careful bite. "I take it you did *not* stand by?"

He sighed and squeezed his eyes shut. "I may have got in a bit of a scrum with his brother over it. A week ago, in London. And I . . . I may have cast a few aspersions on the whole Gyldenkrone family and . . . well, their whole society."

"Cyril!" She sounded horrified, yes—but interested too. She leaned closer. "What did you say?"

"The details hardly matter. The point is that the greve was there while his brother was running off at the mouth, and he *let* him. When I told Emil he oughtn't to say such things, the greve melted into the background, not only making no attempt to tame his brother's wretched tongue, but not even trying to restrain him when he surged drunkenly to his feet and asked if I was fool enough to defend her with actions and not just words." He shook his head, still recalling the disgust on Emil Gyldenkrone's face.

As if *Cyril* was the one saying things no gentleman should say. As if *he* was the cad. As if defending a lady's honor wasn't what one was supposed to do.

Mariah's face went so still, so careful that he knew he'd yet again said the wrong thing, somehow. "What did you *say*, Cyril?"

He frowned. "You're ignoring the point."

"Indulge me."

A sigh leaked out. "Something, perhaps, about how no true nobleman would behave so. And, perhaps, something about how if their society allowed for such things, they . . ."

She winced. "You actually did insult the entire Danish society?"

This conversation wasn't going as he'd planned. "I . . . it was a rhetorical device. Obviously I don't really think . . ."

She shook her head, her gaze dropping to her half-eaten gingerbread. "I suppose one says thoughtless things in the name of love. You must feel quite strongly about Lady Pearl."

"That's not it at all." Even then, before Pearl had sliced him to ribbons, it'd had nothing to do with what he did or didn't feel for her. He shook his head and glanced back to where he knew the manor house hid behind the trees. "I have always been keenly aware that I wasn't born to this. I am no nobleman, certainly not a peer. I'm just a stranger your stepfather had to dig out of the woodwork."

She frowned. "You are not."

"I am. But that's the point, don't you see?" He leaned closer, willing her to understand. "I've had to study. To learn. To discover what this is supposed to mean—what my *life* is supposed to mean, once I realized that so much would be dictated to me. And the only thing I could come to that made any sense—that made the trappings and expectations worthwhile—was the thought that it's supposed to *matter*. That even when so much is handed to us with high expectations, we still have to choose, every day, what sort of person we'll be. We're supposed to seek what's truly noble, truly good. We're supposed to strive to be the best we can be. I know this world is a long way off from the ideals it was founded on, but that doesn't mean the ideals aren't worth trying to attain, does it? That we shouldn't stand up and defend others' honor?"

"Even if they don't deserve it?"

Something about her tone—part challenging, part apologetic—snagged his attention. He frowned. "Are we speaking in general or of Lady Pearl in particular?"

Her mouth twisted to the side. "I know this will sound like jealousy, but we went to school together. I know her well."

A frown tugged at his lips. "She never mentioned you." Which, yes, spoke volumes about Pearl's personality, that she hadn't even mentioned she was acquainted with the daughter of his benefactor—not even when she was hurling her at him like a curse.

Was it amusement in Mariah's eyes? Self-deprecation? Something else altogether? "Of course she didn't. I was never either ally or threat enough for her to notice me."

He breathed a laugh. That sounded like Pearl indeed. "You are now, having stolen her chosen groom."

Mariah looked baffled. "I've done what?"

He motioned toward the house again. "Gyldenkrone. She shouted in my face after I dared to show up with a blackened eye that she was going to marry the greve and go to Denmark and escape us English brutes."

Mariah shook her head, her look of confusion not easing. "But . . . she's chosen *you*. That's why the greve gave up. Isn't it?"

The laugh that slipped out sounded every bit as scornful to his ears as it felt in his chest. "Me? I was never anything but a diversion. A story she could tell. I daresay . . . I daresay the greve gave up because of what his brother so deftly proved. Lady Pearl is no more constant than the fashions she so loves."

If anything, her confused look compounded. "If you believe that, then why did you defend her?"

He spread his hands. "I didn't want to believe it. But more . . . Emil shouldn't have *said* it. Shouldn't have *done* it. No gentleman should behave so."

She pursed her lips, studying him so long that he barely kept from squirming. He was just about to ask whether he'd measured up or been found absolutely lacking when she said, so quietly that her voice was scarcely audible over the cold breeze, "You say you were just a distraction for her. That she dismissed you. You say you defended her more because of Lord Emil than her. And yet . . . you were courting her. And from what I know of you, you're not a man to do so lightly."

Perhaps her words weren't a question exactly, but her expression was. He sighed and toyed with his gingerbread, looking at it rather than her. "I wanted it to mean something—the way Lady Pearl and I met. I thought that perhaps, even if your father didn't really want me as heir . . . even if I couldn't claim you as a friend anymore . . . even if I would feel like a pretender here, that the Lord had sent another means for me to find my place. That perhaps it was His plan for my life. That I could learn the depths she kept from others, that I had something she needed." His eyes slid closed. "I think that's all I've ever really wanted. To belong somewhere, to have a true place, to contribute. To be what someone needed."

When he dared a glance up, he found her expression soft. "You're what we need—all of us here. The one who will let Papa be a father to him. The one who will keep giving hope to the neighbors. The one who will keep this manor thriving. The one," she added, lips curling up and nostrils flaring just a bit, "who isn't afraid to take a promenade through Christmas Wood in search of the magic of yesteryear, lest it make him look silly."

Perhaps she was right. But none of that had felt real to him until he was back here. Castleton had just been a specter of disapproval that haunted him, this place had been unknown shackles, and Mariah . . . Mariah had been a friend who hadn't needed him anymore, who had outgrown the closeness they'd once had. Who had stopped confiding in him or inviting his confidence in her. Pearl had seemed like a story *he* could write for himself. A future beyond what was expected and forced upon him.

What a fool he'd been. She'd been to him exactly what he'd just claimed he was to her—a distraction. That was all. One more excuse to keep from coming back here and facing his fears.

One more thing to keep him from coming home.

Silence fell as they both finished their now-cold gingerbread, but once the last crumbs were gone, Mariah drew in a long breath and offered a bright smile. "Well. Whatever the situation with Lord Emil and Lady Pearl and the trail of broken hearts she has amassed as she promised she would, it's Christmastide, and I have a plan I could use your help with."

He was about to correct her on the broken hearts bit—it was more bruised pride than any heartbreak on his part, and probably far less than that for the coldhearted Dane or his hotheaded brother. But the mention of a plan stole his attention. "Is that a light of scheming I detect in your eyes, Lady Mariah? Ought I go in search of some asparagus swords?"

She laughed and reached into her bag, pulling out a notebook and pen. "Wooden ones will suffice. Here." She fished a few sheets of paper out and handed them to him.

A three-second glance told him what it was. "The play version of our story?"

She nodded, a grin lighting her eyes as much as it curved her lips. "The one the children performed last week. Only, everyone at the manor missed it. Mama and Papa were in Hope, waiting for Fred's train, which was late. Louise begged off, claiming she couldn't stomach it. You hadn't arrived yet. But yesterday, I could tell that the families in the village were disappointed that Papa hadn't been there. The children had been working so hard for weeks, wanting to impress him. A way of thanking him, they said, for all he does for *them* at Christmas."

He lowered the papers. "Well, the answer is simple, isn't it? An encore performance."

"Exactly." But the twinkle in her eyes said it wasn't quite as simple as that. "Only . . . I thought that rather than staging it upon, well, a *stage*, we could use the original backdrop." She waved at the wood.

At Christmas Wood. With its Almond Gate and its Marzipan trees, its Orange Brook leading to Orgeat Lake. He grinned back. "I like it."

"It will take some reworking." She tapped the notebook. "And I was thinking that perhaps we could make it more interactive for our dedicated audience. Lure them into exploring our kingdom like we did as children. Add in a treasure hunt of some sort."

He leaned onto the cold rock of Giant's Table, studying her as she'd just done to him. "Is this really for the village children?"

Her breath eased out in a puff of white. "Partly yes. Partly to bring everyone together once more. But also because . . ." She trailed off, let her gaze sweep the forest. "No one has ever seen things as we used to, Cyril. No one has ever *wanted* to. And more, they keep insisting that I need to put it aside, forget the world of imagination—as if I can't be both a responsible adult and someone who still believes in the impossible."

She straightened, eyes flashing. "But that's what Christmas is about, isn't it? The impossible becoming real. An infinite God becoming a fragile human babe. That perfect God making a path for us to come back to Him, and doing it in a way both spectacular

and yet so mysterious, so hidden that people could and still do deny it. Perhaps if I can help them to laugh and consider, just for a moment, that *this* world is more than it may seem at first glance, then they'll be willing to trust that the world beyond is more too. That the God of hope wants them to believe in the miraculous. Wants them to rejoice with the heavenly choirs. Wants them to truly *live*, not just plod along doing what's expected."

He couldn't help but smile at her. "A reminder I need as much as anyone else. Count me in and assign me my role. I, and anything I have, are at your disposal."

"Well, if you mean that . . ." She flipped the page in her notebook and tapped a heading that was utterly blank beneath it. "I could use some assistance with the battle scenes. We did a fair enough job on a little stage, but with actual space to spread out, I don't think our four paltry jabs will be very convincing."

Cyril grinned. "I know just the chap. Boxing is Kellie's favorite sport, but he's rather a master at other forms of combat too. He trounces me regularly at fencing."

"Your valet?"

"And friend. Yes. He'll be happy to help, I know."

She grinned. "Perfect. And we can sort out how to integrate the treasure hunt and use the props already built here in the wood. But first I need to speak with the families and see if they're willing to stage this encore."

He nodded. "We haven't time to waste then. We'll have to start paying visits to everyone on your list, and inviting anyone not participating directly to be part of the audience."

She gathered her papers and notebook together again. "We should start with the professor. He's always a bit anxious and bored in the days between when he's finished his gifts and installation and the ball. I daresay he'll be happy for something to occupy him."

"To the workshop, then. Unless there's more to plan out here in the cold?"

She shoved her supplies back into her bag. "Now that you mention it, the workshop sounds like just the thing. And I imagine the professor will even offer us some tea."

"Better and better." He hopped off the rock bench and held up his arms to help Mariah do the same.

She didn't need his help. But she accepted it anyway, and then tucked her arm through his in what was swiftly becoming a habit he adored. His heart had never thrilled like this when he walked beside Lady Pearl through London, and the very thought of her here at a country manor, walking through the woods, was nearly laughable.

It made him realize that he'd never actually tried to form an image of the future with her. He'd known, based on everything she said, that she had no interest in a quiet country life, only in the bustle of a city like London—or Copenhagen, perhaps.

And yet he'd known that his primary duties would be to Castleton. To these neighbors Mariah loved so dearly. To representing their needs in Lords someday and doing everything he could to be their friend in the meantime. Even before he'd come back—come home—he'd known that. He'd known this was his future. And known that Pearl would want no part of it.

But with Mariah, he could see the years stretching out before them, imagine season after season with her, discovering each fresh joy.

He cleared his throat, his earlier words marching through his mind, sounding different now than they had then. "Just to be clear—about Lady Pearl."

She stiffened beside him. "Yes?"

"There was never any heartbreak. No love lost. It was the story I was enamored with, nothing more. The chance to be someone's hero. The romance of it all."

"Really." She sounded amused. "Dangerous thing, you know—romance. I've been informed by a very authoritarian Danish fellow that it's a flimsy foundation for something as serious as marriage."

He turned wide eyes on her. "Please tell me that wasn't part of his proposal."

She tilted her head in affirmation, a smile teasing her lips.

"Pitiful." He shook his head as they passed through the gate of their fairyland and exited into the real world again. Real—but still pretty. Still full of joy and promise. "That man needs a few lessons in how to court a woman."

"You ought to offer. See what he says."

He laughed at the very thought. And kept on smiling all the way to the professor's workshop. He might be no expert on courtship himself, but he understood Mariah as he'd never understood Pearl.

Winning her heart would be the only gift he'd ever ask for.

10

Søren hadn't realized it in London, but Cyril Lightbourne was every bit as ridiculous as Lady Mariah. Søren sipped at his tea at the breakfast table on Tuesday morning, stifling the urge to roll his eyes much like Emil would at the laughable conversation the man-child was having now with Lord Castleton.

The earl had brought up a debate he'd been having about what to do with some tenancies in the village of Hope. The population had grown, and he hadn't yet decided where to build new housing.

"Why not ask the villagers where they'd like them to be situated?" Lightbourne had just said in reply.

As if the villagers had any informed opinion about these matters. As if they had studied architecture or the environment enough to weigh in with any authority.

Idiot man.

In the Kingeland home, Lightbourne had been one other suitor standing between Søren and Pearl, more an annoyance than an actual rival. A large annoyance, yes. When he'd happened to be on hand to rescue the lady from the boating accident and then she'd realized he stood to inherit an earldom, she had been far too intrigued.

Lady Pearl, however, could always be counted on to be ambitious above romantic. She enjoyed the story of Lightbourne's rescue, the attention it brought her, both from him and her other adoring admirers. But more than that, she'd craved advancement and position and wealth—something Søren could offer in greater degree than any English suitor. It was really too bad she hadn't shown a bit more discretion when it came to charming, handsome men like Emil.

Irrelevant now, though. Despite the letter he had in his bag from her, declaring that he was the one she'd decided on, and she would accept his proposal the very moment he gave it, Søren had no intentions of ever seeing Lady Pearl Kingeland again.

Lightbourne, on the other hand, he was seeing far more of than he'd ever thought he would, and the increased exposure only made him more convinced this man-child would shoot himself in the foot soon enough. Søren probably needn't bother with any plan more complex than stealing his girl from him.

No doubt to humor his naïve heir, Castleton hummed thought-fully at the suggestion to seek his tenants' opinions on their living situation. "Well now, why not?"

Lightbourne grinned. "They are the ones who live and work there. They must know the land and their own needs better than anyone you could hire in."

Søren took another bite of his toast and meat. The other gentle-men had opted for porridge, but he couldn't stomach the bland English variety, being accustomed as he was to *øllebrød*—rye bread porridge.

If Lightbourne someday joined Lords with opinions like that—*why not ask the people?*—he would make a laughingstock of him-self. Though it would be years before the pup had the chance to humiliate himself so publicly before his peers . . . and though Søren was patient, he wasn't quite *that* patient. Even so, he must tread carefully, as he'd known at the start. A personal humiliation for Lightbourne would be satisfying, but he didn't want to impugn the Castleton family or estate—not when he meant to attach his own name to it.

Which he did. Perhaps Lady Mariah wasn't as beautiful as Pearl, and perhaps her flights of fancy were tiring, but she was sweet-natured. Malleable. Charming, even, in her own way. Not the sort of charm he personally was won over by, but she would be well received by the Danish court, he was certain.

Movement through the doorway caught his eye, and he looked up to catch sight of a feminine form approaching. She really wasn't at all bad to look at either. In fact, her figure was quite beguiling. And viewed in profile like this . . .

No, wait. That wasn't Lady Mariah. It was Louise, Lady Swann, who most definitely did rival Pearl in beauty, despite being seven years her senior. And she was far more sensible than her sister. Perhaps she no longer had a dowry to offer—only whatever widow's portion her first husband had left her—but he didn't need the influx of cash. If she weren't still in mourning and if he weren't after vindication as well as a bride, she would have been the more pleasing choice. But alas.

The sweet taste of revenge more than made up for any lack in Mariah's beauty or sense. He would stick with his original plan both for its logic and that powder of sugar on top.

Louise greeted them softly and moved to the sideboard for her tea and toast. Mariah all but skipped into the room a moment later with the energy of a schoolgirl, placing a kiss upon her stepfather's cheek with a grin. "Morning, Papa. Cyril. My lord. Louise."

Couldn't she at least tamp the enthusiasm down a bit? Mornings and rambunctious greetings didn't mesh.

Castleton and Lightbourne returned her greeting, but her sister sighed and pressed fingers to her temple. "'He that blesseth his friend with a loud voice, rising early in the morning, it shall be counted as a curse to him.' Proverbs—"

"Twenty-seven, fourteen. Yes, I know. You've been quoting it at me since the moment you first read it." She flashed a grin at Cyril. "It was the first verse she memorized, I think. Just for my benefit. I was flattered."

113

"It most certainly was not the first." Louise's lips turned up in the corners, just a bit. It was a shame she didn't smile more—it made her even lovelier. "But without question the one I've had cause to trot out most often."

Castleton chuckled, Lightbourne returned Lady Mariah's grin, and Søren smiled to himself. They were growing closer every day. Anyone with eyes could see it. Which meant it would hurt Lightbourne worse when Søren took her away with him.

Good. Not that he was pleased about the fact that it would upset the lady as well. Though, come to think of it, a little heartbreak could be just what she needed to mature and let go of some of these silly ways of hers. He would be doing her a favor.

And he hadn't been lying on Sunday when he promised her anything she desired in terms of possessions, travel, or benevolence. He would mend her heart with whatever life she wanted. They'd grow fond of each other, just as his parents had done. And once children came along, she would forget any past pain. Given the affection in her voice when she spoke of the village children, he knew she would dote on her own.

"And what are your plans for the day, sweetling?" Castleton directed the question to Mariah as he slathered marmalade onto a triangle of toast.

She flounced to her usual seat at the table, a plate of gingerbread and a cup of tea in hand. "I plan on spending the day in the village. I want to make certain everyone is well before the ball and help in any way I can with last minute tweaks to wardrobe and so on."

Louise frowned at her. "If you're walking to the village, don't you think you had better eat more than cake for breakfast?"

"Who said anything about walking? I was hoping I could take the gig, Papa." She sent him a smile intended to charm him.

Castleton chuckled again. "You know I don't mind in general, but it is a bit slick out there just now. And you remember, I don't doubt, how you handled it last year in the snow?"

Mariah made a sheepish face and glanced outside, where a thin layer of snow had fallen overnight.

Lightbourne set down his spoon. "I'd be happy to drive her, Cass. I have plenty of experience in the snow, and I would love the chance to meet the neighbors."

Søren had far more cold-weather experience than any Englishman could have, but he didn't make an offer of his own, despite the questioning look the earl sent him. No, he simply granted his concession with an inclination of his head.

Let them go together. Let them moon over each other and delight ever more in each other's company. Let Lightbourne tumble even further into the teeth of love. The deeper those teeth dug, the more they would rip him to shreds when Søren and Mariah announced their engagement at the ball.

Castleton gave his approval. The younger two downed their breakfasts and then all but galloped from the room like a couple of children escaping their nursemaid. The earl rose too, declaring he had better go and check on a few things himself.

Søren turned his head toward Louise, ready to make a bit of idle small talk, only to find her frowning thoughtfully at him. "Is there something on your mind, my lady?"

She tilted her head a bit, her food still untouched before her. "Do you think that wise, my lord? To let them go off gallivanting together? I cannot be the only one who sees that neither of them remembers their intendeds when they are together. It is a dangerous thing."

Did she really believe that Lady Pearl had agreed to marry Lightbourne? It seemed she did—that they all did. And he'd let them think it—it would keep the earl from encouraging his favorite stepdaughter to choose him over Søren.

To Louise, he shrugged. "If your sister is the kind to forget herself so fully, I would just as soon learn it now."

Louise blushed. "I do not mean to imply she would behave inappropriately. For all her personality quirks, Mariah is of impeccable moral character. But she once fancied herself in love with Mr. Lightbourne, ever since they met as children. They exchanged letters every week for ages, until my mother put her foot down. Yet they seem to have picked up where they left off. I would think you would want to win her heart from him, not encourage the attachment."

What was it with females insisting upon such sentiments? He felt his brows furrow. "I suppose you think marriage ought to be founded on romance and love too then?"

She pursed her lips. "I think marriage ought to be founded on mutual respect, admiration, and a shared expectation for the future. But Mariah wishes for love and romance. And as she is the one with whom you're considering matrimony, not me, it is her opinion you ought to consider."

He lifted his nearly empty cup and took the last sip of his tepid tea. Put that way, she did have a point. And wouldn't it twist the knife in Lightbourne even more if Søren won not just her hand but her heart? Not to mention that it would make the transition from English miss to Danish mistress easier for her. He set his cup down again, thoughtful. "Your logic is unassailable. But I am afraid I have never given much consideration to making a woman fall in love with me."

When Louise smiled full like she did now, she made Lady Pearl look like a troll. "Lucky for you, my lord, Mariah has bored me with countless versions of her ideal hero over the years. I'm happy to lend you my expertise."

"Generous of you."

She granted it with another tilt of her head. "For all our difficulties, she *is* my sister. I want her to be happy. I think a gentleman like you could be very good for her, if you can overcome her hesitations." She blinded him with another smile. "And I admit I would relish an invitation to visit the two of you in Denmark. The pictures I've seen of it are stunning."

"You would be most welcome to stay as long as you like. My

homes would always be open to anyone in your family." Aside from Lightbourne. That went without saying. But having the coolheaded Louise on hand to calm any of Mariah's outbursts of silliness could be rather handy.

Not that her rebukes calmed Mariah, exactly. But she at least quelled her enthusiasm some of the time.

He poured himself a second cup of tea while Louise recounted the qualifications for a hero that she'd noted as recurring themes in her sister's stories and games. He must be gallant. Handsome. Selfless. Attuned to the needs of others. The sort to rescue the heroine in one moment and yet require her aid in another.

As the list went on, his frown grew deeper. "Your sister wants a man who doesn't exist."

Louise laughed. "Obviously. That is what I've always told her. But the general ideas can be met easily enough. Ask for her opinions and help. Be at hand to lend her your own. Compliment the village children and look for ways to help them and their families. And at least you needn't worry about the handsome part."

He glanced sharply at her at that one and found her blushing slightly. Thanked her with the barest hint of a smile. "We are fortunate that my brother did not join me. When viewed together, everyone always favors him."

"I can't imagine that." Her blush deepened.

He appreciated the sentiment all the more for her self-consciousness over it. "He is . . . charming. Charismatic."

Her eyes went wide, no doubt contrasting the idea with Søren's reserve. "That sounds exhausting. I've found that charming, charismatic men must be watched like a hawk and even then ought never to be trusted. My late husband's brother was much the same, and he left a trail of broken hearts and irate husbands and fathers in his wake." She sighed, shaking her head. "And now the marquessate is his. I have no doubt he will run it into the ground in half a decade, and his poor wife has had to become an expert at turning a blind eye to his indiscretions."

"Deplorable." And he knew exactly how she felt upon considering such a dismal situation. "I pray the Lord grants me a son before anything happens to me. I have no trust in Emil's ability to preserve our legacy for the next generation either."

The lady sipped at her tea. "Why, then, have you not married before now? If you don't mind my asking—please feel free to ignore the question if it is too personal."

"I don't mind." He held his cup in his hands, enjoying the warmth of it. "I was, nearly. Lady Ingrid. Our families had been planning the match for over a decade, but she was a good deal younger than I, so I was to wait for her to come of age. She is, I believe, two years or so older than your sister."

Louise nodded her understanding. "What happened?"

He lifted a shoulder. "Nothing grave. The king and prince summoned me for an audience and shared their reasoning for wanting a stronger alliance with Britain. They suggested I pursue an English bride instead, promising they would arrange another fine match for Ingrid. I had no objections. Ingrid and I would have suited well enough, but we both value our relationship with the royal family above all. Neither of us even considered objecting to their recommendation."

"Sensible."

"Indeed. She is betrothed now to another greve—older even than I, a widower who was without an heir. She will be a boon to his family. Just as your sister will be to mine."

"All's well that ends well, then." Her smile was more muted, though, than it had been before. She glanced at the watch pinned to her bodice. "I had better return to my knitting. If I may make a suggestion—perhaps you ought to explore the village? One never knows when my sister could slip or fall and need a helping hand up."

He returned her muted smile, stood, and took the liberty of scooting her chair out for her so she could stand. "Thank you, my lady, for your help and advice. I am in your debt."

Her smile this time looked more sorrowful than ever. "That

remains to be seen, I think. But you are most welcome, regardless. I wish you good luck with my sister."

Søren thanked her and bade her farewell, hastening to his room to change into his riding habit. The earl had already offered him a mount anytime he felt the need for a ride, and he had only to wait a few minutes in the stable for a fine sorrel mare to be prepared for him.

The ride to the village was short, brisk, and did wonders for clearing his head. He ought to have taken some exercise before now. He'd kept up with his usual calisthenics in his room, but he'd missed the invigoration of outdoor exercise.

Castleton wasn't so large that it should prove difficult to find Mariah and Lightbourne, and he saw their gig quickly enough. Empty, but they must be in one of the row of shops.

Reasoning that a quick survey of the town could be useful, he kept his horse moving, filing away every detail he saw. Later, he would add his impressions to his journal, along with a few sketches of the town.

In a town this small, he garnered a fair share of attention. More than one woman out with her children paused to gape up at him, and quite a few men paused in their work to stare. Ordinarily he would have ignored them, but Louise's advice rang in his head.

He smiled, tipped his hat, even called out a few "Happy Christmas" greetings, all of which were heartily returned. He didn't need the people of Castleton to like him. But it couldn't hurt if they chattered to Mariah about what an amiable fellow he was.

By the time he'd finished his circuit and returned to the village square, Mariah and Lightbourne were exiting one of the shops and hurrying toward another. Perhaps, had they not been laughing together, they would have noticed him dismounting from his borrowed mount. As it was, the only thing Mariah seemed to notice beyond her companion was a bakery window. She paused, pointed, and even from across the square Søren could hear her exclamations of pleasure and joy. Rather than go in, though, she pulled herself away, and she and Lightbourne ducked into another shop.

Søren strode to the bakery window, toying with the idea of buying her something. Women liked gifts, didn't they? And she had a sweet tooth—she seemed especially fond of the seasonal delights of Christmas. How was he to know which of the biscuits and cakes and confections had caught her eye? And what if it had been the massive gingerbread house dominating the display? He could hardly cart that back to the manor house on his horse. Besides, he'd seen most of these same treats on the trays that had been included with every meal and tea.

An idea percolated in his mind. Yes, these traditional English treats were already on hand at the manor house . . . but he knew a few confections that most assuredly weren't, and that wouldn't be found in any English bakery either.

And to be honest, he rather missed the taste of his own traditional baked goods, enough that he'd considered asking the cook at the manor to bake a few of them before deciding against it. A good guest never asked for what wasn't readily offered. And he certainly didn't want to appear to be a sentimental fool. He'd contented himself with a review of the recipes he had written down in one of his old journals and the knowledge that when he returned home in the new year, he could ask his own chef to bake them.

Decision made, he pushed into the shop, a bell heralding his arrival and the scents of sugar and yeast and spices greeting his nose.

A plump fellow with a flour-dusted apron stepped from the back kitchen to the front sales area, his eyes going wide as Søren strode toward him. "Em . . . good day, sir. You must be a visitor to our fair village. To Plumford, perchance?"

"Quite right." He smiled, telling himself to try and imitate the way Emil did it. "Lord Castleton and his family have been quite welcoming."

"Oh, they're the best sort, they are indeed." The baker's tone was warm, and his shoulders relaxed a bit.

Good. Still imitating his brother's relaxed demeanor, Søren leaned onto the glass display case. "I wonder, good sir, if you are available to help with a holiday scheme of mine?"

"Scheme, you say?" His eyes darted toward the door, uncertainty coloring them.

Søren chuckled. "Nothing underhanded, I promise you. I only want to surprise the Castleton family with some confections from my country. Denmark."

"Ah." The shadows fell away from the man's eyes, but he frowned in the next second. "I don't believe I have any Danish recipes, I'm afraid."

"I have a few." At the way the baker's brows flew up, Søren shrugged. "I have an excellent memory and write down every new thing I learn. Last year, I gifted my own chef with a very lovely printed book of classic recipes, and I read through it myself first to make certain it was appropriate. I copied out a few of my favorites." Oh, how Emil had scoffed at him when he'd come in and found him about it. He would never, his brother claimed, have any need for those recipes, so why had he bothered?

But what was so comical about studying the things one liked best? It had helped him to realize what common ingredients he favored most, and hence why he was drawn to the dishes he was and steered clear of those he didn't. He could now tell his chef "no anise, but anything with almond paste is acceptable" and know that he would never have to send a dish back.

And besides, writing down one's favorite recipes might even be called whimsical, mightn't it? Mariah would certainly find it so and would appreciate the effort he was going to now.

The baker pursed his lips. "Well now, sir. I'm happy to help, if I have the ingredients on hand. Could you copy the recipes out for me now, do you think? Or send them along later?"

"I can copy them for you now, if you have some paper and a pen or pencil."

Ordinarily he would have referred to his journal to guarantee accuracy, but he had just reviewed those recipes yesterday. The memory was fresh and clear.

The baker watched as he wrote, nodding encouragingly and muttering things like, "Ah yes, a classic pastry crust. I've plenty of butter and flour on hand, of course. . . . Yeast! An interesting addition. Give it a bit of a puff, I'd think. Delightful."

By the time Søren finished, the chap was beaming. "Not a problem at all. I can't guarantee the presentation will be exactly what you're used to, mind you, having never seen them. But the processes look familiar enough, and the taste ought to be right. What do you call this, now?"

"Kringle."

"Looks like a bit of rest time for that dough . . . but I can have them prepared for you by this afternoon. Though if I may offer a suggestion?" The man looked up from studying the recipe.

Søren nodded slightly.

He tapped a finger to the instruction to fill it with a tart cherry jam. "I happen to have several jars of plum preserves made from the earl's own fruit. It's a favorite of theirs. I don't see why it wouldn't work in this just as well as cherry."

His first instinct was to refuse—after all, the mixture of cherry and almond filling was what made it say Christmas to him. But remembering Louise's advice—*selfless*—he reconsidered. Something or another with plums had been at nearly every meal, which he hadn't bothered to notice until the baker drew his attention to it. It made sense, though—the vast plum orchards dominated the estate's southern acres. The earl and his family were proud of their fruit in all its forms, so much so that the entire estate bore the name. Wouldn't using their own preserves gain him even more favor?

He nodded. "Brilliant idea. Please make the adjustment as you see fit."

ROSEANNA M. WHITE

He left the bakery again more than satisfied. Emil would call him smug. And he might be right. Setting himself to follow his soon-to-be-betrothed, he smiled to himself. He'd steal her if he must. Win her if he could.

And either way, Lightbourne would be wallowing in sorrow this Christmas instead of joy.

11

Mariah led Cyril into the carpenters' shop, still laughing over the jokes he'd been exchanging with a couple of the school-aged boys who were freshly on holiday and hence out in the streets, chasing mischief about. The soothing scent of wood shavings greeted her, as did the familiar voices of Joe Green and Jack Smith.

"Lady Mariah! Happy Christmas."

"Well now, to what do we owe this considerable honor?"

"And if it isn't the young Mr. Lightbourne too!"

Mariah's grin shifted to a quirked brow at that last part. "Have you met?"

"Unofficially," Cyril said from behind her. "Kellie and I had the honor of helping right an overturned cart of Christmas greenery on our way to the manor. How do you do today, gents?"

"Oh, fine, fine," Mr. Green said. "Finished the last of our commissions for Christmas yesterday, so mostly just whiling away the time before we close up the shop tomorrow."

"Oh good. You're available, then." Mariah stepped past the desk where customers sat to discuss their needs and into the workshop, catching a glimpse of what she was hoping would have been stored there—the Almond Gate that they'd crafted and painted with far more care than she'd expected. And the rest of the stage sets were there too, making her clap her hands together in delight. She'd been half-afraid they would have been taken apart already. "I was hoping to put your magnificent props to use again."

Mr. Smith and Mr. Green had both trailed her the few steps into the workshop, and Mr. Smith now patted one of the gates but kept his gaze on her. "Another play? So soon?"

"Part encore," Cyril supplied with a grin from his place in the threshold to the shop. "Part embellishment."

Mariah laid out her plan—how she wanted to give the children the chance to put on their play at the manor, not only for her parents but for the visiting Danish lord, and how she hoped it would brighten the holiday for everyone, especially if they lured the audience into participating. "Do you think your children will be game? I even found someone to coach them in the battle scenes that gave us such trouble before."

Both the men chuckled. "A chance to put on the show again, better even than before?" Mr. Green gave her a what-do-you-think look. "Try and keep them away. Mine are still talking about it every moment and bemoaning that his lordship and her ladyship missed it."

"Ours too," Mr. Smith agreed. "They'll clamor at the chance, I know it. Though you can ask them yourselves if you stick about for a few minutes, I daresay."

"Oh good." Mariah gave them each a grin. "We've spoken to a few of the other families on our way into the village, and the vicar was agreeable when we stopped in to see if he was available to be our narrator again, given that the performance would be Christmas Eve afternoon."

Mr. Green nodded toward Cyril—or perhaps to the front door behind him. "There comes Suzanna now, and the children with her."

Suzanna Smith—sister of Mr. Green and wife of Mr. Smith—entered the shop with a flurry of wind-blown snow, her three rosy-cheeked children skipping in with obvious joy at being released from their lessons for Christmas. Mariah had always thought Suzanna one of the loveliest women she'd ever seen. Tall and willowy, her face as exquisite as Louise's—and her disposition a good deal more prone to fun. She was one of those women who was even more beautiful now, in her mid-thirties, than she had been at twenty, when Mariah first met her.

If only life treated all of them so well.

Mariah greeted Suzanna and the children heartily, listened to the younger ones chatter about their grand Christmas plans, and let them try to ply information from her on what Professor Skylark had up his sleeve this year—making a show of buttoning her lips at that one. And when they met her silence with exaggerated groans, she laughed and leaned forward.

"You know I can't tell you that—but I do have a favor to ask, which I hope will be a special treat for you as well." Seeing the way their eyes lit up at the thought of a conspiracy, she grinned. "Mr. Lightbourne and I have decided that we should put on our play again, but at the manor this time—and not just on a stage, but over the grounds. What say you?"

The children were an immediate cacophony of enthusiastic agreement, scarcely standing still for details before dashing out to secure the cooperation of their friends.

Suzanna chuckled as they left. "I predict your entire cast will be gathered for another rehearsal within a quarter hour."

"Do you think they'll be able to come for an official one this afternoon?" Cyril had tucked himself out of the way but eased forward a step now. "Lady Mariah mentioned that the swordfighting scene could use a bit more choreography, and I've drafted my valet to act as instructor."

"I daresay the mums and das will be glad to have the little ones out from underfoot for an hour or two." Mr. Green grinned. "And I wouldn't mind coming along to observe. Call me a chaperone. Or a helper. Whatever you need."

Suzanna frowned, the look more one of question than uncertainty. "You mentioned the performance spanning the estate. Would you like some of the parents to come along to shepherd the children and keep them in their proper places? I know you handled them backstage last week so we could enjoy the performance, but even you can't be everywhere at once, my lady."

She hadn't given that any thought, but Suzanna had a point. She nodded slowly, the idea forming and bringing a new smile to her lips. "That would be helpful indeed, since you've seen it already. Although . . . I think it'll be more effective if you're in costume too."

The woman's brows lifted. "Us? But—"

"I have a number of gowns I've found in the attic that should work splendidly. I found them when I was searching for items we could use for the play, but they were too big for the children. They'll be perfect for you and Jane and Martha, though, especially if I can talk Mrs. Roy into making a few last-minute adjustments."

Suzanna looked caught halfway between excitement and doubt. "But the gowns in your attic will be from previous countesses. It doesn't seem quite likely that anything would suit us."

"Nonsense. In fact, I unearthed a beautiful purple gown that should fit you perfectly. You can be a fairy guide."

Her lips twitched into a smile. "A sugar plum fairy, from the sounds of it."

"Exactly so." A laugh bubbled up. This would be even better than the original play. If parents volunteered to help direct the children, then it meant most of the village would be involved. What better to remind her parents of how beloved they were? "I'll pay a visit to Mrs. Roy straightaway and will send the gowns to you as soon as I get back to the manor. Could I put you in charge of the other mothers and their costuming?"

"Of course. We were planning to have tea together this afternoon anyway."

"And just tell us when to haul the props up to the manor and where to set it up, and we'll be there," Mr. Smith added.

As Mariah and Cyril exited the shop a few minutes later, she couldn't help but smile. She'd hoped everyone would be eager for another performance, but there had been the possibility that everyone would be too busy tomorrow, and she certainly hadn't wanted to impose on planned family time.

The streets were now abuzz with children shouting happily over getting to don their costumes and play their parts again, excited all the more when Cyril promised them that Kellie would arrive after tea to train the soldiers on the village green—and that they ought to bring sticks or toy swords with them. The girls were pirouetting as if in their costumes again already, ignoring the talk of mock sword fights. Georgette Green and her friends rushed up to inform her that they were going to add a few decorations to their snow-fairy costumes.

"I can't wait to see your work," Mariah pronounced with a tap on each cold-pinked nose. "You were the loveliest snow fairies I have ever seen."

"Mama made us each snow crowns," Victoria Nithercott said, presumably for Cyril's benefit. "From tin foil and white sequins and paper lace doilies."

Cyril gave a solemn nod, eyes alight. "As every snow fairy should have, clearly. I can't wait to see it. I was heartbroken to have missed the play, when Lady Mariah told me about it. Did you know I helped her write that original story when we were children?"

Victoria's eyes went wide. "Did you? You know the *real* Christmas Wood, then?"

He laughed with delight rather than anything patronizing. "Are you kidding? It's my very own realm." He struck a dashing pose. "I'm the original Prince Nutcracker himself, you know."

That was enough to send the girls into renewed giggles and shouts. "Now you've done it," Mariah said softly as the children darted off to rejoin their friends. "All the little girls will be mooning over you. They decided during our rehearsals that Prince Nutcracker was the noblest, dearest hero ever to be conceived."

His cheeks went pink.

It made her heart warm to see it. To see him here, interacting with the people who would someday be his tenants. Laughing with the children. Plotting with the parents. Being a part of the village, and loving every moment.

She had never doubted that he'd make Castleton his home—not as he had. She'd always known that when he came back, he would be coming *home*. She just hadn't known how it would touch her heart to see how excited he was about their old story-turned-play, or the way everything inside her would go bright and warm as she watched him so quickly find his place.

She hadn't dared admit to herself in recent months how much she'd wanted to see just this. Him. Here. How much she yearned to see him here for years to come. How much she wanted to stay here, too, for the rest of her days. Not go off to Denmark, or to any other place in England, for that matter.

But Cyril wasn't a brother or even a close cousin that she could just impose on. He was Papa's heir, yes, and her friend. But neither of those things was enough to give *her* a true, long-lasting place at Plumford Manor. Only one thing could do that—something she'd forced herself to write off as an impossibility.

By the time they'd made their visits—though by the end, word had spread and half the village was already gathered again—morning had turned to afternoon and teatime was approaching.

Mariah's stomach was growling as they neared the little stone-and-brick bridge over the river Esk. Their last visit had taken them to one of the cottages on the far side of the ice-coated river, but they needed to return to the gig in town before they could drive home.

Cyril chuckled, either at the noises rumbling from her abdomen or at the heat that stung her cheeks at such an unladylike announcement of teatime's approach. "Perhaps we should have accepted one of those offers of luncheon."

Mariah shook her head. "We had far too many visits that needed made to take the time to eat with any one family." But now that they'd ticked the last one off their list, contentment seeped into her veins. "A day well spent, I think."

"Agreed. My only regret is that we didn't drive out to this last one." He'd been the one to suggest the longer walk, so she frowned at this pronouncement. She wasn't so hungry that the extra five minutes to walk and then drive back over the bridge was really any inconvenience. "Seems we have a troll blocking the way."

At that, she turned to the bridge, not knowing quite how to respond to the vision that met her eyes.

Lord Gyldenkrone stood at the crest of the small arched bridge, holding his horse's reins with one hand and a telltale baker's box in his other. He was watching them, waiting for them—and not minding that doing so blocked the narrow bridge.

Not that there was any traffic waiting to get by him. Even so, Mariah picked up her pace. If he'd stationed himself there so that he couldn't miss their arrival, then he would move and clear the way after he'd said whatever he meant to say, and she didn't want them to be an inconvenience for anyone who might need the road. Though why he didn't just wait to find her until they were back at Plumford she couldn't guess.

Cyril sighed and increased his stride as well. "Usually people don't run to meet the troll, you know," he mumbled.

She sent him a chiding, if amused, look. "Do behave yourself, Cyril."

"Must I?"

Rather than answer, Mariah smiled and closed the distance between them and their Danish guest. "Good afternoon, my lord," she said once they were near enough. "What brings you to Castleton today?"

"A special errand." He smiled—actually smiled, in a way that looked not only genuine but . . . apologetic? Sheepish?

"It occurs to me—" he darted a glance at Cyril, hesitated,

and then looked back to Mariah—"I owe you an apology for the brusque manner in which I broached the subject of my court-ship on Sunday. I pray you can forgive me. For so many years now, responsibility has been the byword for my every thought and consideration. I haven't spared any time for matters of the heart, nor considered how to approach them. Your sister took me to task for that this morning, and she was absolutely right. You need—deserve—to be more than a choice made from logic and responsibility."

Mariah could only blink, agape, for a long moment. In her shock, she didn't know where to begin. On second thought, yes she did. "Louise said that?"

Lord Gyldenkrone nodded. "And I am not fool enough to ignore sound wisdom when I hear it, nor too proud to admit when I was wrong. Please, Lady Mariah, can you forgive me for my coldness the other day?"

Cyril shifted beside her, and she could feel the tension radiat-ing from him, just as she could hear the barely whispered "What is he up to?"

Her spine straightened. She couldn't quite imagine accepting the greve's proposal and going with him to Denmark in two short weeks, but she wasn't about to snub a man who was seeking to do the right thing and apologize for his past behavior.

She took a step away from Cyril, toward Gyldenkrone. "I forgive you, my lord. And thank you, besides, for demonstrating such care now for my feelings."

He ducked his head a bit in a move so boyish that she had to blink to make sure she'd seen correctly. He indicated the box he held, tipping up its lid. "A peace offering? I had the baker make some traditional Danish treats for you—well, for everyone at the manor. But especially with you in mind. I've noticed how you love holiday sweets."

Intrigued, Mariah took yet another step toward him, close enough that she could peer into the box. Her mouth watered at the beautiful golden pastries cut into diamonds, some delicious-looking fruit filling oozing out and icing glazed on top. "Oh, that looks divine. What is it?"

"Kringle. It's baked in the shape of a wreath, but that seemed difficult to layer in the box with the amount he made, so the baker and I agreed he would go ahead and cut it into portions. Traditionally a cherry filling is used, but we decided to use plum preserves instead. From your own orchards."

Her eyes went wide with delight, especially when the breeze brought its fragrance to her nose. "It smells amazing."

"Try a piece. Please. I admit to already tasting one at the bakery. He did an impressive job, especially when one considers that he'd never even heard of kringle until this morning when I gave him a recipe."

She reached into the box and pulled out a delicate piece of pastry. "You had a recipe?"

He shrugged, looking a bit sheepish again. "I am what my brother calls 'a fiendish journaler.' I record everything, including my favorites from a recipe book I gave to my chef last year."

The admission made Cyril's frown deepen, but Mariah found it rather endearing. She didn't know any other gentlemen who bothered to write down recipes for their favorite dishes. She took the first bite of the plum kringle, and her eyes slid closed in joy. "Oh, this is beyond delicious."

Gyldenkrone held the box out to Cyril. "Would you like one, Mr. Lightbourne?"

Cyril didn't even glance down at them. "No. Thank you."

An unexpected, sharp frustration surged up in her. Gyldenkrone was trying to be nice. Why couldn't Cyril embrace the Christmas spirit enough to accept this peace offering that obviously cost the greve a bit of his pride? "Try one, Cyril," she said. Prodded, really. And perhaps her tone had absorbed a bit of her frustration. Perhaps that was why he bristled.

"Haven't you learned anything from fairy tales, Ri? When

a crone offers you something tasty-looking, you're wise to refuse." His tone was light, joking, but his eyes were hard and calculating.

She flushed, her lips parting in surprise. It was one thing to joke about fairy-tale villains between the two of them, but to say it aloud to Gyldenkrone himself?

The greve frowned. "I don't know this word. 'Crone'? From context, it's a villain of some sort, and I can appreciate the similarity to the ending of my own name, but if you mean your insult to land, Mr. Lightbourne, perhaps you ought to define the term for me."

Mariah's cheeks burned even hotter. "A crone is an old witch—and Mr. Lightbourne ought to apologize for saying such things."

"Mr. Lightbourne would rather demand an explanation." He took a step closer to the Dane, eyes narrowed. "What are you really about, Gyldenkrone?"

"Apologizing." But the flash of his ice-blue eyes said he knew well Cyril wasn't asking about this exchange in particular.

Cyril ignored him, spreading his arms wide. "Is this about the brawl with your brother? Is that why you've followed me here, to obtain some sort of revenge? Well then, take it. Take your best shot. Leave Mariah out of it."

Gyldenkrone let the box's lid fall closed again. His face smoothed out into its usual stony, impassive planes. "You think far too highly of yourself if you presume that *you* are my reason for asking the lovely Lady Mariah to marry me."

The words seemed to ricochet off Cyril—but they then pummeled Mariah over the head. Was that what this was about—part of it, at least? Was he after not only her family connections, but revenge on Cyril for the brawl with his brother, the slight her old friend had placed on his family and country?

Heat surged up so fast it nearly blinded her. Of course. Of course that was it. None of this was really about her. Not Gyldenkrone's attention. And Cyril . . . Cyril was only out to best the man he deemed ignoble. Prove him even more so, even now, even with *her*. What was it he had said about the brawl? That it hadn't been about Lady Pearl, it had been about Emil.

This was certainly the same. Not about her—never about her. About *them*.

"And this," Cyril said, motioning to the pastry box and Gyldenkrone and his horse, "is obviously just one more step in your plan. Make her like you. Win her over with sweets and apologies."

The greve frowned. "Certainly that was my intent. Yes, my lady, I hoped to win a bit of favor with sweets and apologies. If that is so wrong of me, then I will beg your forgiveness yet again. I wasn't aware that saying I was sorry was a sin."

"It isn't." Her words were little more than a murmur, lost under Cyril's next accusation.

"It is when you do it for the wrong reasons. You aren't trying to win her for the sake of winning her. You're trying to win her to get revenge on me."

Because she was his friend? Or had Gyldenkrone suspected there was something more to their relationship—the very thing she used to dream it would be?

She tried to tell herself that it was the sudden gust of icy wind making her eyes sting, but even she couldn't believe that fiction. The stinging was too hot, too wet. Too blurring. Was it so inconceivable that a man of Gyldenkrone's status would care just a bit about her opinion?

Cyril clearly thought so. And if that was what he thought, it was a wonder he didn't go on to point out that it was a useless endeavor, because why would he care whether she married some heartless Scandinavian man and moved away forever?

She spun and prepared to run, to push past Cyril and dash the mile home.

She didn't have the chance. The heel of her boot caught on an icy cobblestone, but she had too much momentum to slip and right herself. Her foot went out from under her, half-eaten kringle flying. She had just enough purchase remaining from her other foot to give herself a bit of direction, so she aimed for the solid stone of the sides of the bridge. It would be embarrassing, but it would catch her.

A miscalculation, which she knew the moment her hands landed. The stones, too, were icy, and her palms flew off them, her torso folding over the railing but finding no purchase either.

No. No, no, no, she wasn't going to fall over this dratted bridge! She felt momentum carrying her over and reached for anything she could, and her fingers managed to catch one of the seams between brick and stone. It caught her, slowed her just enough to stop her from tumbling headfirst into the icy river.

But her legs had already followed her top over the side, and their weight proved too much for her precarious fingerhold. With a scream more of protest than fear, she lost her grip and tumbled down.

The drop wasn't far. And the river wasn't deep. This time of year, the Esk had only a foot or two of water in it as it wove around Castleton. But it was coated with a thin sheet of ice that she broke through, and that was enough to throw off her balance. Her knees buckled, and her rear broke through the ice too, inviting a sluggish surge of ice-cold water not only into her boots but into her lap.

"Mariah!"

"My lady!"

She would have called up that she was fine, but they could obviously see she wasn't injured—other than her dignity—and her teeth were already chattering so fiercely that she feared no words would be intelligible anyway. She saved her energy instead for pushing to her feet.

The water came only to her mid-calf once she was standing, but her dress and coat had soaked in enough of it that she was dripping from waist to hem. And the ice had only broken where she'd fallen. The edges of the river were still frozen over, and how was she supposed to cross to the sides? Either direction was only three feet away, but it looked about a mile just now.

The men had raced down, both of their faces masked in horror. Both were jabbering, but she didn't pay any attention to their words. Just to the arms stretching out from the bank toward her.

Gyldenkrone was the taller, which meant his arm reached farther. She stretched out her own, able to grip him and let him grab onto her arm, then, once halfway secure, reaching to Cyril with her other hand. Between the two of them, she was back on solid, slippery ground in another few seconds.

"We need to get you home posthaste," Gyldenkrone said.

"I'll get the gig."

"The horse will be faster and is right here." Gyldenkrone's larynx bobbed with a hard swallow. "The two of you can take it. I'll fetch the gig."

Cyril shook his head. "I'm not much of a horseman. She'll be better off riding with you."

Gyldenkrone hesitated only a moment. Then, with a nod, he scooped her up into his arms without asking if she actually needed such assistance—which she would have felt obligated to turn down—and darted back up onto the bridge. Within a minute, he'd gotten them both onto the mare and was galloping toward the manor.

"I'm sorry," the greve whispered only when they slowed as they came in through the gates. "I never intended you to get hurt."

He meant more than the shivers, she suspected. And she could only pray her answer spoke of more too. "I'll be fine."

12

Cyril trudged through the door of Plumford Manor with the winter's early night following him in, step by heavy step. He could only nod his thanks to the doorman and hand off his hat and cape, his lips unable to form words.

If only they'd had good enough sense to be silent three hours earlier. He handed off the box of pastries that Gyldenkrone had left forgotten on the bridge, trusting that the man would know to whom they should be delivered in order to be added to the evening's dessert trays.

The doorman inclined his head. "The dressing gong sounded about ten minutes ago, sir."

"Thank you," he managed to eke out between his cold lips. That gave him fifty minutes before he would be expected to join the family and make polite conversation.

It felt like a quest of Arthurian proportions. He had too many apologies vying for their chance to be spoken to leave any room for idle chitchat. And he'd had all afternoon to reject one wording after another.

To Gyldenkrone, yes. He shouldn't have acted as he had on the bridge. It had been jealousy that had spurred him on, pure and simple. Because he'd recognized as surely as Mariah had that apologizing as he'd done—in front of Cyril, no less—had cost the man a great deal of pride. He'd done the right thing. He'd made a peace offering.

Even if he did have not-so-stellar motives behind it, of which Cyril had no proof, he had still done the right thing—and it was wretched of Cyril to have tried to make it about himself instead of Mariah.

Because even if Gyldenkrone had followed him here seeking some type of revenge, he was too honorable a man to punish Mariah on his behalf. Even if it had started that way, he was no doubt half in love with her by now. How could he not be? She was everything sweet and lovely.

But Cyril's petty lashing out had instead made her feel insignificant, used, unwanted. He ought to be drawn and quartered for such a crime. Or at least left in some old-fashioned stocks or something. It would serve him right if she refused to speak to him again altogether.

Not feeling up to the number of stairs required to reach his room—he had Kellie to thank for the physical exhaustion that rivaled his emotional one, after the afternoon's "training" of village men and boys—Cyril turned toward the library instead. He knew well there would be a fire crackling in the hearth, since this was Castleton's favorite room in the evenings, and indeed there was. He sank into one of the leather chairs nearest to it and sighed, staring into the flames.

He would have to apologize to Gyldenkrone. And to Mariah. If only he knew how to make the words enough. If only he had a way to wind back time and undo that ridiculous exchange on the bridge. He should have tucked his own pride away and accepted the peace offering. He should have tried, somehow, to offer friendship to the Dane instead of contempt.

That was the kind of man Mariah deserved—the kind whose heart was as big and as golden as hers. The kind who made friends of enemies, not enemies of friends. The kind who was big enough to forgive and Christlike enough to walk an extra mile for someone who had never shown him even a scrap of kindness. It was the kind of man he wanted to be, had been trying to shape himself into.

He had a long way to go.

Raking a hand through his hair, he closed his eyes and offered up a prayer that was more silent groaning than words, that the Lord would show him how. How to be worthy of Him. Worthy of her. How to convince her to give him a chance when he kept ruining things with his own insecurities and childish jealousies.

"Well now. Don't tell me you decided to go wading in the Esk today too. You look as forlorn as Mariah did when she went upstairs."

Cyril looked up at Castleton's increasingly familiar voice, but he couldn't manage a smile. "Is she all right?"

Her stepfather certainly wouldn't be chuckling as he claimed the chair across from Cyril's if she weren't. "Nothing a hot bath and change of clothes couldn't fix, though her mother insists she stay in the upstairs sitting room with her blankets and a good book this evening rather than joining us for the meal."

Was that relief or disappointment swelling in his chest?

Disappointment. Definitely. Hard as it would be to apologize, seeing her would always be better than not. "Would Lady Castleton object if I dropped in to apologize to her? I feel terrible for my part in the afternoon's misadventure."

"You may—though I don't see what blame you could possibly take on yourself. Mariah said she slipped and tried to steady herself on an icy railing, and that was that."

Of course she wouldn't tell him *why* she'd tried to run on an icy bridge—she was too good to cast blame on anyone else. But his guilty conscience writhed. "It was my fault. I upset her, and she meant to storm off to be rid of me."

Castleton's good humor didn't entirely fade, though he frowned. "You've piqued my curiosity, I confess. From what I've seen, the two of you have picked up right where you left off with your friendship from childhood. Don't tell me you're still bickering as you did then too?"

Bickering? Cyril's brows crashed together. And with their joining, forgotten memories sprang up behind his eyes. Yes, they had bickered, as children always did when their enthusiasm took different bents. They'd argued over which path to take in the wood, whether today they would act out the fairy world part of their story or the battle again. Whether they wanted hot chocolate or tea to drink when they came inside.

The quick, inconsequential arguments of childhood that had felt insurmountable for the half hour in which they roared . . . and then were forgotten before the clock could chime again, as they chased the next adventure together. That sort of bickering hadn't carried over into letters, but minor conflict was part of being *with* someone. Of sharing space. Of mixing ideas.

Cyril sighed. "Not exactly the same sort of bickering. I insulted her."

"How so?" Castleton sounded baffled, as if he couldn't conceive of anything over which his favorite could be insulted.

He was right about that. Cyril waved a hand before resting his head on it. "I meant to insult Gyldenkrone—which I also shouldn't have done. But I made it sound like she was unworthy of his court on her own merits."

Castleton's wince looked empathetic. He sighed too. "It's a tricky thing, I grant you, these society matches. Mariah is charming and beautiful, and that is ultimately what will win the heart of her future husband. But one can't discount that decisions are made for more logical reasons and that softer emotions often have to run to catch up. Poor Mariah—that reality doesn't rest easily on her shoulders."

"No."

Silence pulsed, stretched out by the crackling fire for a long minute. Then the earl turned inquisitive eyes on him again. "Why would you have meant to insult the greve? A bit of leftover antagonism from when you were both courting Lady Pearl?"

"I . . ." He shifted, the supple chair suddenly uncomfortable. "In a way, I suppose."

Castleton shook his head. "Time to let that go, I should think. You've won your lady. Let him choose another without butting heads."

Cyril squeezed his eyes shut for a beat. Apparently Mariah hadn't shared the truth he'd told her yesterday, which oughtn't to have surprised him. Though he rather wished she had, just now.

"I haven't, though. Won Lady Pearl, I mean—and don't want to. The truth is, my lord, neither of us was ever really fond of anything but the story of our meeting. She dismissed me last week . . . and I'm glad of it."

Bemusement and understanding mixed in Castleton's eyes. "So why, then, this antagonism between you and the greve?"

Cyril dragged in a long breath. "To be honest, I'm none too keen on him pursuing Mariah when I . . . when I would like to do so myself." No need to bring up his suspicions about Gyldenkrone's motivations, nor the honor he'd been so convinced was lacking. Regardless, Cyril had no room to judge.

"When you . . . ?" The bemusement gave way to a sparkle in his eyes. "Well. Why didn't you say so, old boy? I may not have been so quick to encourage Gyldenkrone's suit if I'd known you inclined that direction."

The old adage about honesty and best policies knew what it was on about. He pinched the bridge of his nose. "She was very clear from the start that friendship was what she desired between us. I'd hoped to convince her otherwise, but I fear I've shot myself in the foot with my behavior today."

"Oh, bah." Castleton leaned forward, a smile dancing over his lips though he tried to tamp it down. "Mariah isn't one to hold a grudge. Tell her you're sorry, state your intentions, and win her over. Nothing would make me happier."

He made it sound so easy. "And . . . you would give your blessing? You approve of Gyldenkrone and already granted *him* your blessing—"

"Because he is a fine man, if a bit cool for Mariah. As are you—the fine bit, not the cool bit." Castleton spread his hands. "I only want her to be happy and well loved. Whoever she chooses, that is all that matters to me."

That's what Cyril wanted too. But up until this afternoon, he'd have been willing to bet that Gyldenkrone did not have those same interests at heart. Now, though?

The man had done something thoughtful. And had been just as shaken by her fall from the bridge as Cyril had. And whether he still harbored any animosity toward Cyril or not, he'd shown himself the bigger man today.

His throat felt tight and dry. "Do you know where I might find Gyldenkrone? I would like to apologize to him too."

"I believe he and Fred were finishing up a game of billiards before dressing for dinner."

"Thanks." He pushed himself to his feet, urging a bit of speed into his step in the hopes of finding Gyldenkrone in the main part of the house and not having to venture out to the bachelor wing in search of him. Now that he'd decided to apologize, he didn't want to wait.

Luck was with him. He passed Fred in the corridor outside the billiards room and found the greve just inside it, about to follow Fred out.

Cyril stepped inside and cleared his throat. "Could I detain you for a moment, my lord?"

The greve paused, and curiosity filled his eyes. "I suppose."

Another long inhale was required before he could begin. "I . . . owe you an apology. Several of them, actually. First for my rudeness this afternoon. It was uncalled for. I have no reason to question your motivations in pursuing Lady Mariah. She is certainly worthy of any and all attention."

The muscle in the Dane's jaw ticked, but he made no reply.

Just as well. Cyril rushed on. "More, I must apologize for my arrogant thoughts, as you so aptly called them. You were right. I thought far too highly of myself, attributing your arrival here to me and my brawl with your brother. I hope you'll forgive me for those selfish assumptions."

Now Gyldenkrone's fair brows tugged down.

Cyril pressed on. "But most of all . . . I must beg the forgiveness of you and your brother. I let my temper and affront lead me to an insult as grave as the one your brother gave to Lady Pearl. I maintain that his behavior, both in luring her into an embrace and then in bragging about it, was wrong. But I shouldn't have slurred your family and nation as I did. I will write him a letter of apology this very evening, and I will do what I can to rectify any damage I did to his reputation."

The silence stretched so long that it crackled and wheezed in his ears. Cyril was about to give up and turn when Gyldenkrone finally let out a short puff of breath. "You needn't bother—with mending Emil's reputation, I mean. I had a wire from him this morning. He has already returned to Copenhagen. I don't imagine he'll be returning to London anytime soon, and by the time he does, one evening's drunken brawl will not be remembered."

Cyril shook his head. "That is not the point. I was wrong. You demonstrated today that you are a people of honor. I would be remiss in my own if I didn't share that observation with any who will listen."

Gyldenkrone took one step toward the door but then paused. "You . . . are not who I thought you were either. I accept your apology, sir, and will offer my own. Because you weren't entirely wrong. You were not my sole reason in pursuing Lady Mariah—but I would be lying if I said it hadn't played a part in my decision." He strode out into the corridor then, leaving Cyril to gape after him.

He hadn't been wrong? But . . . what did that mean now? Were his intentions still so muddled when it came to Mariah? Or did he mean to step aside?

He didn't know. And honestly, it didn't matter. His own pursuit of that most worthy lady ought to be independent of any concerns of Gyldenkrone. He would try to win her heart on his own merits, not by casting aspersions on his rival. Just as she deserved to be loved for her own.

And he knew the perfect place to start.

He flew along the passageways, into the service corridors, already mumbling apologies to every single person he passed, knowing he was in their way during one of the busiest times of day. Though when he reached the kitchen, everyone bustling about seemed to be in surprisingly good spirits. They even had a gramophone set up, with Christmas carols spilling out.

Mrs. Trutchen turned and spotted him the moment he stepped inside, her face lighting up. She hurried over to him, motioning toward the white baker's box that rested on a workbench. "Thank you for the pastries, sir. They smell delightful. Are they for the pudding this evening?"

"I imagine so. They are actually courtesy of Lord Gyldenkrone. Only, he forgot them in his haste to get Lady Mariah home this afternoon. They are a traditional Danish Christmas treat, I believe."

Her expression shifted yet lost none of its brightness. "Lovely! Perhaps I'll see if the baker will lend me the recipe so I can try my hand at them."

"His lordship has the recipe himself. He's the one who shared it with the baker." Cyril smiled, wishing it were easier to give the man the credit he was due, but trusting that, with practice, the ease would come. "Though I did wonder if I could abscond with one of them now? Lady Mariah won't be coming down for dinner, and I'd like to replace the one I made her drop earlier."

The cook chuckled and plucked out a perfect diamond of pastry, setting it on a dainty plate. "Any other time of year, I may feel the need to caution about ruining one's supper. But it's Christmas, after all. I hope she enjoys it."

"As do I." He said his farewells and then backtracked to the main part of the house, finding plenty of energy now to climb the stairs and move to the hallway that contained the family's bedrooms. There, between the rooms she and her sister occupied, he spotted the small, feminine sitting room with its cozy sofa and crackling fire. Lady Mariah nestled into the cushions, her hair in a simple braid that hung over her shoulder, and a thick blanket tucked over her legs. A book rested in her lap, her fingers poised to turn a page.

He'd never seen a more beautiful sight.

Though the door stood open, he rapped a knuckle upon its frame anyway. "Pardon me, my lady. Have you time for a bit of groveling from an oaf of a man not deserving of your forgiveness but who dares to ask for it anyway?"

She paused, looked up, and smiled. Not quite as brightly as usual, but she smiled. "Cyril. Come in."

He did, choosing the chair at right angles to her sofa. He set the plate on the small table between them. "A peace offering."

She tilted her head. "I believe that was Lord Gyldenkrone's peace offering."

"Exactly. I oughtn't to have questioned it as I did. I've already apologized to him."

"You have?" That clearly surprised her.

Frankly, it surprised him too. He wouldn't have thought, as the Cyril who'd made his stand in London, that he had it in him.

But he was a different Cyril here, with her. A better version of himself. Or he wanted to be, anyway. Thought he could be, with her warm heart to show him the way and help him better understand what the Lord wanted of him.

He nodded. "For many things. For today, for my assumptions, and for what I said about his brother and family at the Marlborough. So now I must apologize to you."

She swallowed, her gaze never leaving his face. "Not necessary. I know you meant no insult, and it wasn't your fault that I slipped."

He reached out to rest his fingers over hers. "Don't be so easy on me. I may not have meant the things I said to hurt you, but I still said exactly what I meant. And that was wrong of me. I should have given him more credit, and certainly should have given *you* more credit."

The fact that Gyldenkrone said he hadn't been wrong was irrelevant. Wrong or right, he shouldn't have let his suspicions reflect on her.

Mariah drew in a long breath and let it slowly out. "No, I think you were right. There was nothing about *me* that brought Lord Gyldenkrone here. He meant no harm to me—he was genuinely upset by what happened on the bridge, I could tell. But I can't fathom why he thought the way to antagonize you was through me."

Couldn't she? His lips wanted to twitch into a grin, but if he set it free, he would just blurt out here and now that obviously the greve could see in a moment how Cyril loved every single thing about Mariah.

That wasn't how he wanted his confession of his feelings and intentions to be given—on a random evening in her sitting room, while she still chased off the chill of his stupidity. She deserved more than that.

She deserved magic.

In response to her question, he simply said, "Well, I think it's irrelevant. If I'm not mistaken, Lord Gyldenkrone has already been softened a bit. After our little adventure tomorrow, he's certain to be a bowl of bread pudding."

And as long as that oh-so-soft greve didn't direct that hidden sweetness to her and somehow win her yet with his change of heart, they'd be fine. Cyril had a bit of his own plan brewing . . . and he'd spend the night plotting and praying and hoping.

13

Mariah turned in front of the full-length mirror, unable to hold back a smile. The gown for this evening's ball had turned out beautifully. She'd already turned slowly to examine it from every angle and had declared to Mrs. Roy that it was the most gorgeous thing she'd ever worn.

Mrs. Roy had smiled in pleasure, whispered that the other projects were done and in the hands of their recipients too, and then had gone to make certain Mariah's mother and sister had no last-minute adjustments needed for their own gowns. Blakely had trotted off with her to assist Louise.

Which meant no one was watching.

Feeling a sly grin settle onto her lips, Mariah curtsied low to the mirror, pretending she saw Cyril in it instead of herself. "I would be delighted to give you this dance," she whispered to his imagined question. Left arm raised as if resting on his shoulder and right hand holding up the long skirt with its short train, she hummed her own music and waltzed about her bedroom.

It was going to be a good day—no, a *magical* day. It was Christmas Eve, and she'd awoken with a heart warm and thrumming and ready for delight. She'd sneaked outside at daybreak and found Misters Smith and Green already in the wood, their children laughing with them, setting up the play's props—all but the Almond Gate, which would be too visible from the house. Those would come later.

The children had decided that the best way to be certain the guests traveled the right paths throughout the adventure would be to position themselves strategically around the wood. The boys, already in the grey clothing of their mouse costumes and one of them even with a tail on, had chosen spots by potential wrong turns and were planning to toss acorns and snowballs at passersby to keep them from entering.

"Gently," young Theo Green had solemnly sworn. "We'll only frighten them off. We'll aim for their feet."

"And we," Georgette had added, spinning about in her snow fairy costume, which looked positively darling, "will guide them on the right path." Then she'd come to a halt, bounced on her toes, and grabbed Mariah's hand. "You ought to see Mama! She looks so pretty in her gown!"

Of that Mariah had no doubt. Just as she had no doubt that Louise would outshine *her* at the ball. But as she pretended to dance with Cyril, none of that mattered.

Because she would dance with Cyril tonight, and it would be twelve years' worth of dreaming coming true. Even if he stomped on her toes or she spilled mulled cider down her front, it would be perfect.

She'd lain awake long into the night, staring out the window at the few pinpoints of starlight visible before clouds obscured them, praying and thinking over the choices she had to make. She tried to imagine herself accepting Gyldenkrone's proposal, traveling with him to Denmark, leaving England behind. Leaving Plumford behind.

She couldn't. Much as his reaction yesterday had helped her to see his warmer side, that very revelation made it clear to her that he wasn't the husband the Lord had for her. Because even as she'd looked into his repentant blue eyes, even as he begged her forgiveness as they hurried back to the manor, all she'd wanted was *Cyril's* apology. Cyril's repentance. As the greve had helped her from the horse and rushed her into the warmth of the house, she'd wished it had been her old friend's arm steadying her.

She hadn't meant to remember every dream she'd ever dreamed of Cyril. She hadn't meant to fall in love with him even before he confessed that he'd never felt anything but wishful thinking for Lady Pearl. She hadn't meant to give in to the blasted convenience of it all.

But it had taken only a few hours of his company to remember why he'd been her dearest friend for so many years, even when they had only letters to connect them. The distance of the last four couldn't erase that, especially when that gap was bridged so easily now.

It wouldn't be fair to marry Gyldenkrone when she felt this way about Cyril, even if Cyril never saw *her* as anything but his childhood friend.

And so tonight might be only an illusion, a magical pretending that faded back to ordinary after the holiday. But for tonight, she was going to let herself dream. Tonight, she wouldn't know yet if he'd never want her as she wanted him. Tonight would be all potential. It would be Christmas, and that was something no circumstance could take away.

However the day went, it would end at ten till midnight, and their ball would stop, and the vicar would step forward and lead them to the manor's chapel. They would hear the story, again but always anew, of Christ's coming. They would sing her favorite hymns.

It would be Christmas. Magical—no, *miraculous* Christmas. The day when heaven had come down to earth. The day when the stars sang out His glory, and the angels with them. The day God Eternal wrapped Himself in delicate human flesh and put His feet into time.

Today would be a beautiful day, and tomorrow too. No matter

what happened, no matter how wrong things went, no matter how her silly little plan of fictional adventure fell through, it would be beautiful.

"Oh, Mariah. How I envy you."

She nearly tripped, not just at Louise's voice suddenly intruding, but over that strange note in it. Mariah halted, spun, and spotted her sister leaning into the doorway that Blakely had left open. Louise watched her, not with her usual disdain, but with . . . wistfulness.

Mariah frowned. "I can't think why you would." Louise also wore her gown for the ball, and it highlighted every perfect feature that her sister had.

Yet her sister's smile was small and sad. She pushed off the door and moved to sit on the edge of Mariah's four-poster bed, her gaze never leaving Mariah's face. She shook her head. "I don't think I ever . . . I don't remember ever being so free as you looked just now. So . . . light. Bright."

Mariah hesitated. Just for one moment, or perhaps two. How many times had she tried over the years to really talk to her sister? To shower her with affection? To make them friends? But Louise had rebuffed her and chided her and always left her feeling more alone than before.

And yet never before had Louise sat there with such vulnerability on her face. How could Mariah not try, just one more time? She moved swiftly to sit beside her sister, even daring to reach out and weave their fingers together. "It's no secret that we are very different. But that's no reason you can't be free."

Louise shook her head, even that action looking elegant and graceful. "I always resented you so."

"Resented me?" That wasn't the word that Mariah would have thought fit the situation. She would have said she annoyed her sister, that she frustrated her, disappointed her. But *resented* made it sound as though it originated in Louise's heart, rather than in Mariah's own flaws.

"You didn't remember. Within months of Father's death, you . . . you forgot. You were too young." Gaze unfocused now, Louise stared into a past Mariah couldn't see. "I know you were only two when he died, but I hated that you forgot him so quickly. He was my favorite person in the world. Fred remembered at least a little, but you . . ."

Mariah frowned, but what else could she do? Apologize for being too young?

Louise didn't wait for her response anyway. "And then Mother married Cass, and before the first year was out, you were calling him Papa. And you were laughing again and twirling about and telling your silly stories. You were happy. You were always happy, and I . . ." She squeezed her eyes shut, and her lips trembled. "I never stopped missing him. It tinged everything."

Throat tight, Mariah took Louise's hand into her lap and forced out a question. "Why are you telling me this?"

Louise's head bowed. "I thought life would grow brighter when I married Swann." Not an answer, but Mariah didn't push. Perhaps her sister was working round to something. "We were a good match. Well suited. I . . . I know you think me heartless, but I did love him. Perhaps it wasn't why I chose him, but it came quickly."

"I never thought you heartless." Not convinced her sister even heard her, she squeezed her fingers too.

"I thought once I had a family of my own, I'd be able to shake the old sorrow. But instead, new sorrow found me." Tears dripped down Louise's cheeks. She didn't even wipe them away. "First the stillbirths. Then Swann himself. Why, Mariah? Why has grief and death dogged my every step?"

Mariah had no answer, and she didn't think her sister honestly expected her to have one. She let go of her hand and wrapped her arms around her instead, resting her head on Louise's shoulder. "I don't know. But I do know that a woman of lesser strength would have buckled. Not you, though. You are so strong, Louise."

"I'm not. I'm . . . brittle."

"You're strong. And you're inspiring. I know we disagree on our approaches to life, but I have always looked up to you."

The breath of laughter that puffed from Louise's lips sounded more incredulous than amused. "No you haven't."

"Of course I have. My beautiful, perfect sister."

"Hardly. I'm a dusty old widow well past my prime."

Mariah's laugh was also more incredulous than amused, if a good deal brighter. "Are you jesting? Fishing for compliments? Louise, you are only twenty-six, and without question still the most beautiful woman in London. You put that ghastly Lady Pearl to shame. Crook your finger and you'll have men falling at your feet again whenever you're ready to wade through them."

"You exaggerate."

"I don't! Do you know that the only time Lady Pearl paid me any attention at finishing school was on our last day, when she took it upon herself to interrogate me as to whether you would be rejoining society this last Season? She was in dread that you would be, and that she'd be competing with you."

For a moment, Louise looked flattered—or, no. Just startled. Genuinely surprised at the thought that a debutante would be intimidated by a widow so much her senior. Then even that melted back into malaise. She shook her head. "I admit that I miss society. That I miss the company of a husband. But the thought of competing for one again holds no allure."

"Well look at that. Something we can agree on."

Louise smiled. A real, true, albeit small smile. Aimed at Mariah. Over something she said.

She'd count it as the first miracle of Christmas.

Her sister drew in a long breath and rested her head against Mariah's. "You'll not have to navigate those waters again. I hope you realize how fortunate you are, little sister. Lord Gyldenkrone is one of the finest men I've ever met. He'll be good for you and you for him."

Did she dare to risk this fragile peace by contradicting her?

Not quite yet, anyway. Better to firm up its foundations a bit more first. "He told me what you said yesterday. How you advised him to offer kindness instead of logic."

"Well. Not my exact words . . . but you're welcome." She sighed out the breath she'd just pulled in. "I do want you to be happy, Mariah. And I . . . I don't want to see you ruin your chances with Lord Gyldenkrone over this old attachment you have to Cyril. He's a fine enough young man too, don't get me wrong, but he's already engaged."

"He isn't, actually." That didn't mean he had any interest in Mariah as a potential wife. But a friendship like theirs could so easily grow into more. She had to believe that. It might take some time, but if she could artfully worm her way out of any expectations with Gyldenkrone, there was still hope.

And the way her sister spoke of the greve . . .

Mariah narrowed her eyes. "Louise . . . one can't help but notice that *you*, in fact, would be better suited to Lord Gyldenkrone than I. And honestly, the thought of a husband who has already agreed with you more than with me is a bit exhausting."

Louise looked caught between dismissal and amusement. "I know it's difficult for you, Mariah, but don't be silly. He came to England looking for a young bride with a dowry and family connections. Not an old widow with nothing to her name but her name."

"You are not old! I do wish you'd stop saying you are, because I have no intention of granting that *I* am in a few years."

Louise waved that off and straightened from her lean into Mariah. "Don't fill my head with nonsense. It's you he's after. Not me. And that's . . . that's as it should be. It's your turn, little sweetling. Mine has passed and isn't likely to come round again."

She wanted it to, though. Never in her life had Mariah understood anything about her sister so clearly. She really did admire the greve, and this decision on her part to help him win Mariah . . . it was a brave, selfless thing she was trying to do. To give to Mariah what she herself most desired.

Love surged up for this woman with whom she'd been at odds her whole life. Mariah captured her hand again and held it between her own. "You're a good sister." Her lips curved. "But so am I. Don't give up hope yet, Louise. I think the Lord has a happily-ever-after in store for you yet, if you're bold enough to seize it."

Her sister narrowed her eyes. "What are you up to now?" Her voice, however, didn't sound suspicious like it usually would have. It sounded curious.

Mariah just grinned all the more and stood. "I think we had better get out of these ball gowns."

"I suppose you're right. We don't want to wrinkle them." Louise stood too and moved toward the door.

"Louise?" When her sister paused and looked back, Mariah pursed her lips. "Dress warmly. I have a feeling we may end up outside this afternoon."

"In the snow?" Louise sounded disbelieving as she glanced out the window.

It was snowing? Mariah spun around, a gasp of pleasure slipping out when she saw the beautiful flakes drifting slowly down. "Oh! Perfection! Well, that seals it. We must go out later! Oh, I hope there's enough to break out the sleigh."

"That does sound festive." Louise sounded begrudging. "All right. I'll dress warmly. Should I caution Mother to do the same?"

She couldn't quite believe that her sister would accept her advice without demanding to know what she had up her sleeve, but perhaps the conversation had left her feeling warm toward Mariah too. She nodded. Waited for Louise to move to her own room, or to Mama's. Waited until she heard their voices.

Then she darted out into the corridor, down to Cyril's door, and rapped lightly upon it. She had no idea if he was there or if—"Oh!"

His valet, Kellie, opened the door, looking startled to find her there.

Cyril was right behind him, then elbowing him aside. His eyes

154

were wide as they swept her from head to toe. "Mariah. Wow. Your costume for the day?"

She laughed at the idea—not ashamed to admit she was delighted by the response. "Don't be silly. For the evening. I'm about to go and change. But first . . . a slight tweak to the afternoon's plans." She leaned closer so she could pitch her voice low. "We need to orchestrate things so that Gyldenkrone and Louise end up together during the adventure."

"We do?" His surprise quickly gave way to understanding, and then a smile. "Quite right. That makes much more sense."

"Doesn't it just?"

"They're rather perfect, really. I mean, they'll be doubly insufferable together. But perfect."

She laughed and stepped away. "If you make it outside before I do, give the instruction to Mrs. Green and the children."

He saluted her, stiff as a toy soldier, but for his wide grin.

Mariah darted back to her room just as Blakely made her way to it as well. As her maid helped her out of her exquisite ball gown and into the pretty, warm clothing Mariah had chosen for the day, Mariah let her smile—and her plotting—fade.

Better to pray than to scheme. Pray that the Lord would breathe life upon them today. That just as He had sent the ultimate miracle to earth on this coming night so long ago, He would send a smaller one now to their family.

That He would show them true joy. True peace. True love of family and neighbor. That somehow, through the whirl of snow and music of laughter, they would see what she so dearly prayed they would.

That joy didn't come from what the world said made sense. Joy came by embracing love.

14

*T*he sentimentality took Søren off guard—and kept him in his room all morning. He'd awoken with a strange, tense feeling in his chest. Strange enough and tense enough that he'd been alarmed. Was he unwell? Something wrong with his heart?

He'd lain there for several minutes, sounding out his muscles and limbs. He'd risen carefully, done his usual morning calisthenics, and had realized that it wasn't his physical self that ached. It was, inexplicably, his inner self. Emotional? Mental? Spiritual? He hadn't been certain.

So he'd sat down at the small desk in his well-appointed guest room and he'd pulled out a few leather-bound books. First, the Bible that he always carried with him on his travels but rarely opened—he had many key passages memorized already, so it seemed superfluous on many occasions. Secondly, the journals he'd packed.

It was Christmas Eve. It was Christmas Eve, and for the first time in his life, he wasn't in Denmark for the holiday. How strange that this should cause such a pang when he thought of it. How strange that he sat there for no fewer than ten minutes, blinking through three decades of memories and wishing he were home. Wishing Emil were at his side, poking and prodding and cajoling

him into having fun. Wishing, even, for memories yet to be made
. . . memories that would bring life to the dream that still lingered
even after he awoke from it.

A dream of a family gathered around the hearth in his own
home, his own Christmas tree towering above them. A dream of
the laughter of children and the smiling face of their dark-haired
mother. A wife he didn't have. Not yet.

He'd stared at the Bible, another strange feeling overtaking him
as he flipped open its thin, crisp pages. Familiar Danish words
sprang out at him as he flipped toward the Gospels, soothing a
few of the ragged edges even as that new feeling burned hotter.

He knew the words in this Book. He'd read it through five
times, front to back. Because it was a good thing to do, even an
expected thing to do. Because a favorite cousin of the very devout
Lutheran king must know his Scriptures backward and forward.
Because they were as true as any textbook or history. Because it
was what one did.

Yet here, now, on Christmas Eve in a foreign country, at a house
he'd come to with vengeance in mind as much as any noble motives, those reasons felt flimsy and dull. Tarnished.

He felt tarnished, when all his life he'd worked so hard to be
sterling. Golden. Worthy of his family name.

He hadn't just come here seeking a bride. He'd come seeking
revenge for an insult to his brother that had been deserving, if
not kind. He'd come determined to make Cyril Lightbourne pay.

His father would have been appalled. His king and cousin too.
He should be appalled that he'd considered even for a moment
using Lady Mariah as a means of revenge against Cyril Lightbourne.

The conviction had sliced him through as he watched Lady
Mariah tumble over that icy bridge yesterday. He hadn't really
paused to think about how short the fall was, or how low the
water. And even after he'd realized it, it hadn't made his regretful
heart thud any less violently. If she hadn't slowed her tumble and

flipped herself, that low water could have spelled her doom. She would have gone down headfirst into that shallow, icy trickle. She could have broken her neck. Been paralyzed. Been killed.

And for what? His anger over someone calling Emil exactly what he was? His desire to win Mariah as much for spite as because she'd been a reasonable choice? Even though he didn't *want* her to be his wife?

That realization hadn't come yesterday, though. No, it was the one he woke up to, disorienting as it was. Hers hadn't been the face in his dream. Nor had Ingrid's, though there would have been logic to that.

It had been Louise there in his unconscious imaginings.

He didn't know why his mind had gone that direction as he slept, but when he considered that today was the day Lady Mariah ought to be giving him an answer on his proposal, dread curled in his stomach. Not that she might refuse—but that she might accept.

He didn't want to marry Lady Mariah Lyons. Even more so because he'd realized yesterday that she was, in fact, a sweet and charming young lady with a heart of gold. She didn't deserve to have that heart broken, despite his thoughts yesterday morning. She didn't deserve to be his means of revenge.

And revenge rang rather hollow after Lightbourne's sincere apology last night.

It was one thing to hold a grudge against an arrogant, insufferable blighter. Quite another to hold one against a good-hearted, humble man whose main flaw was being young.

He wouldn't always be young. But he could always be good-hearted, if the world didn't pummel it out of him.

Søren had decided, at some point in the night, that he didn't mean to be part of the pummeling. Not anymore. He wasn't so petty. Or at least, he didn't want to be. Something about Lightbourne's admission that Søren had proven himself the bigger man that day did him in.

He hadn't been, not really. He'd only wanted to look like he was. But Lightbourne had met his counterfeit humility with the real thing, and he'd recognized the difference in himself. He'd seen that the younger man had achieved in truth what Søren had only pretended to.

That wasn't who he wanted to be. It wasn't honorable. Wasn't noble. Wasn't worthy of his name or his family or his king.

Certainly wasn't worthy of the King they were celebrating today.

He read the familiar Nativity narrative in Luke, even though he knew many of the words by heart and would no doubt hear them at church tonight as well, albeit in English. He read it again just to cement it in his mind, and then he spent the next several hours with his journals, ignoring the grumbling of his stomach.

He would feast later, with the family. First, a bit of fasting to punctuate his repentance. It seemed fitting.

By the time he was satisfied with his self-reflection, it was one o'clock in the afternoon—he'd missed luncheon too, but that was all right. He felt, for the first time in years, light. Clean. Like the fluffy mounds of snow pillowing the world outside his window.

His lips turned up. A white Christmas, at least, as Christmases ought to be. He hadn't dared to hope for such a thing in England, where it was just as likely to be a drizzly and foggy one, but the snowflakes dancing down felt a bit like a kiss from heaven. A promise that no matter how frozen and hard the ground of his heart had been before, it could be made pure and sweet again.

A knock made him spin for his bedroom door. No doubt it would be a servant, inquiring after him on behalf of the earl, perhaps seeing if he needed a tray of food. Perhaps even Castleton himself, making certain he was well.

He grimaced a bit at that one. He'd have to talk to the earl sometime today. Confess that he didn't think he was a wise choice of husband for Lady Mariah after all—and encourage him to encourage Lightbourne to pursue her instead. That would be the right thing. The kind thing. The good thing.

Neither a servant nor their employer stood at his door, though. It was Lord Lyons, a winter coat draped over his arm and hands shoved into his pockets. He looked caught halfway between glum and curious. "Afternoon, Gyldenkrone," he said.

Søren nodded. "Good afternoon. And Happy Christmas."

"Right." The ladies' brother half turned away. "I've been sent to fetch you. We've been summoned downstairs and instructed to dress warmly."

Søren gripped the door rather than move through it. "Summoned by whom? To what purpose?" New leaf turned over or not, a man couldn't just be expected to trot merrily off without a few details.

Lyons shrugged. "I received my instructions via Cass, but I got the impression Mariah was behind it. So brace yourself for something ridiculous."

Was that how he had sounded, even yesterday? Søren smiled. "I believe the word you're looking for is *delightful*. A bit of Christmas whimsy sounds like just the thing."

The young lord rolled his eyes. "Not you too. You seemed perfectly reasonable last evening."

Chuckling, Søren fetched the outerwear he'd taken up here with him yesterday rather than handing it off to a servant below. "Let's just say I've realized that I can appreciate her perspective."

"We'll see about that, I think. She's also invited any of the servants who could slip away from their duties for a few minutes."

Unusual . . . but it *was* Christmastime. To recognize one's staff and even grant them extra time off from their duties wasn't so uncommon. And considering that tonight's ball was for the entire region, rich and poor alike, how could he be surprised by this news?

He shrugged and followed Lyons down the corridor and toward the main part of the house. His guide asked him a few polite questions about what he'd usually be doing on Christmas Eve in Denmark, and Søren answered with fuller answers than he would have done any other day.

Talking about home made him miss it more. And yet also made him look forward to the festivities here. He would be forming new memories, which he would be able to regale his friends and relatives with back home. Perhaps he could even exaggerate here and there to make it sound as though he'd had a sort of Dickensian Christmas experience, his heart made soft by an epiphany. A Christmas miracle.

Or maybe it wouldn't require much by way of exaggeration. As they gathered with the others outside the ballroom's closed doors and he spotted Lightbourne guarding the entrance with a grin, he had to admit that the animosity was gone. Just . . . gone. That had to be a miracle, didn't it? How could he really have purged his heart on his own, so quickly?

He gazed over the crowd of family and servants, searching for Lady Mariah. There were more people here than there had been yesterday, and he suddenly remembered a mention of some more distant relatives arriving today. He had a feeling she would consider it an early gift for him to rescind his proposal and remove from her shoulders the burden of sorting out how best to let him down. But if she was here among the throng—there had to be seventy people gathered outside these doors!—he didn't spot her.

He spotted Louise, though, standing off to the side with her hands clutching her elbows, arms folded across her middle. She looked a bit lost, and though he'd only known her a few days, that struck him as out of character.

"Excuse me," he muttered to Lyons, who didn't seem to mind that he abandoned him, and slid his way through the crowd until he'd come up beside Louise.

Odd. Never in his thoughts had he called her Lady Swann, though he ought to have. That was interesting, wasn't it?

"Happy Christmas, my lord," she said in greeting, perking up a bit as he neared. Her smile, however, looked strained. "We missed you this morning. Though I suspected you were planning your next step in wooing my sister. She's to answer you by the ball, correct?"

Was there a note of something in her voice? Dread? False cheer? Or was that only wishful thinking on his part?

He shook his head. "On the contrary. I was repenting of ever asking her, when it's so very clear that we're not well suited. The scare yesterday convinced me that she's too sweet a girl to be forced into a match like I could offer. She will be better off with Lightbourne. And I . . . I think I will be better off with a wife who possesses a steadier head on her shoulders and a bit more maturity. Your sister is charming, but charming alone isn't what I seek."

Louise blinked at him, her lips parting, but she had no chance to put voice to whatever thoughts swirled through her lovely blue eyes. At that moment, piano music boomed enthusiastically from within the ballroom, and the matching French doors swung wide under Lightbourne's hand.

"Enter," said a voice from within, resounding over the piano with authority and drama—wasn't it the vicar's voice? He hadn't sounded so theatrical behind the pulpit on Sunday, though. "Enter to a world of terror and delight. Of dastardly villains and heroes so bright. Enter to a world of magical things . . . of miracles and mayhem and the hope to which we cling. . . ."

Søren moved inside with the others, careful to stay close to Louise's side. He heard some of the staff murmuring that those were the opening lines of the children's Christmas play that they'd performed in the village the week before, someone else adding that they must have decided to stage it again so that the Castletons could see it. He didn't know why that would require a winter coat, though. And, to be honest, the prospect of sitting through a children's play sounded boring.

But he had to blink in wonder as they entered the ballroom. When he'd seen it last, it had been already bedecked for Christmas, yes, but not like this. Now, dozens of paper snowflakes seemed to drift in midair from whatever strings on which they dangled. Candlelight turned to gold the snow-softened light that poured in through the windows, and the scent of cinnamon and cloves spiced the air. There were no chairs set up for the audience, nor an invitation to make themselves comfortable.

The piano went softer, turning from thunderous announcement to a playful tinkling of keys. That must have been some sort of cue. Figures he hadn't noticed emerged from where they'd been curled under chairs or beside tables, twirling out onto the floor in a dance whose enthusiasm outshone its choreography. The village children, he realized. Mostly girls, though there were two or three lads among them.

They acted out a scene of Christmas gift-giving, the little ones belting out their lines with confidence. They were telling a rather typical tale of a holiday party, boys and girls at odds, eventually fighting over a large nutcracker doll that Professor Skylark presented to them. It broke during the argument, and the professor mended it.

Søren shifted from one foot to the other. Why had they not brought chairs in for them? Was there not space enough in the ballroom for this audience, perhaps? He felt a bit of familiar irritation creeping in but shoved it back down. The village families had gone out of their way to create this encore production of the play the lord and lady of the manor had missed. It spoke of these neighbors' dedication to one another. Which said volumes too about the kind of landlord Castleton was. The kind of family this was.

He glanced down at Louise. From what he'd gathered in the last several days, she had declined attending the original performance for reasons he'd not heard. But the look on her face now was of longing as she watched the little ones. Longing and a gentle sort of joy. He found himself smiling simply because of how it softened her lovely features.

Just as the rest of the audience began shifting impatiently, as the drama wound down and the children pretended to be sent off to bed in the play, a sudden bugle call had them all jumping. Children again swarmed forward, some dressed as mice, others as toy soldiers. The lead soldier, dressed like the nutcracker doll, called out a challenge to the "vile mouse king," and a battle clashed.

Søren grinned at the very dramatic—but rather well choreographed, he noted—battle that ensued. Both mice and soldiers jumped about, thrust, parried. He caught sight of an adult at the side of the room giving muted directions that probably weren't meant to be heard over the music and narration, but the concentration on the fellow's face made Søren smile still more. Lightbourne's valet, wasn't he? He mocked a few thrusts and parries, nodding to the children.

At last, the largest of the mice, who wore a tinfoil crown upon his head, was facing off with the nutcracker boy. Their antics were even more exaggerated than the others', earning more laughs and gasps from the audience. He was certain they were about to thrust each other through when the piano went thunderous again, and the doors out onto the porch sprang open.

He hadn't even noticed the adults who had crept up outside to open them, but he was fairly certain as he watched them jump away again that Mariah was one of them. Not surprising, he supposed, if this was her doing.

Both mice and soldier hordes had been circling the audience and, once behind them, must have begun delivering a few prods to those in the back, given the squeaks of protest, giggles, and shouts of "Onward, onward! You must help in the battle! Into Christmas Wood!"

Ah, the portion of the play that required their outerwear. Søren slipped his overcoat on and then assisted Louise with hers, offering her a smile—and then his arm.

Their guides got more insistent once everyone had bundled up, urging them outside. The vicar's parting words carried after them. "Go, go into Christmas Wood! Through the Almond Gate as Prince Nutcracker would. Find, find the magic he seeks, that will make him a man and defeat the vile Squeaks! For somewhere in his kingdom a present is hid—will you find it first? Oh, you'll wish that you did!

Look for a box wrapped in gold bright as sun, and at Orgeat Lake show your prize to the ones who have written this tale for your Christmas delight. The gift will unlock further joys this fine night."

"Oh, a treasure hunt! Jolly good!" Castleton tugged his wife out through the doors and into a trot that had the lady squealing and laughing. "Come, love. Let's find it, whatever it is!"

Søren led Louise out into the swirling snow behind her parents, though rather than take off for the wood as the others were doing, he instead steered her toward where her sister stood grinning against the side of the house, no doubt poised to close the doors again after her guests had exited.

Lady Mariah's smile only grew when they drew near. "Oh, good! I was hoping you both would join the fun. Though I wouldn't dawdle—Papa seems pretty bent on finding that golden package."

"I only wanted to take a moment first, to save you some trouble." He cleared his throat, making a point of looking at no face but her own—he owed her that. "You needn't sort out how to turn me down this evening, my lady. Don't let it cast a shadow over your day. You were right. I've come to understand that. Consider my offer rescinded and . . ." Now he glanced over toward where Lightbourne stood sentinel at the next door. "And I wish you a bright and happy future."

He expected a bit of surprise at least. A widening of her eyes, or visible relief. What he didn't expect was the hand she held out, businesslike. "You're a sensible man, my lord. I knew you'd see reason. I wish you every happiness as well." She had no compunction, it seemed, about darting her own gaze to her sister. "And I wish you success in your mission."

He couldn't recall ever shaking a lady's hand before—a clasp and a kiss was the standard, after all—but he shook hers, the corners of his mouth lifting in a grin. He had a feeling she knew exactly what his new mission was. And he would take all the well-wishes and prayers he could get. "I thank you for that. Happy Christmas, Lady Mariah."

She grinned again. "Enjoy the adventure, my lord. Louise—you too. Please."

He led Louise away then, into the fluff of fresh-fallen snow, away from the tracks others had already put down. Yes, he saw the strange "gates" shaped like almonds positioned directly ahead, but if they were to end up at the small lake—he had to assume that was the one they'd renamed so whimsically—then why not take a bit of a shortcut?

Louise was silent for several minutes, and he let her digest everything that had just transpired. Before she finally spoke, she delicately cleared her throat. "Well. I'm surprised, my lord. And, I confess, disappointed. I did so hope to have an excuse to visit you in Denmark."

He was beginning to understand Mariah's perpetual smiles. His own lips refused to return to a neutral position. "I was rather hoping you still would."

Her laugh was dry. Sad. "I daresay Lady Pearl won't appreciate that."

"I daresay Lady Pearl has no right to an opinion, given that I never intend to speak to her again unless our paths cross by happenstance."

Finally, she looked up at him, confusion on her face. "But if you've decided against my sister and Lady Pearl . . ."

"If you recall, my dear Louise"—A risk, yes, that liberty of calling her by her first name, but he prayed she'd forgive him—"I said before this delightful adventure began that I needed a woman with *more* maturity, and with a steady head on her shoulders. I was rather thinking . . . hoping . . . praying that I may convince *you* to entertain the notion of a courtship."

She came to a halt, her eyes not only wide but—tearful?

He sucked in a sharp breath. "Forgive me. I meant to cause you no distress. If it's still too soon after the loss of your late husband—"

"No!" She rested a hand briefly on his chest, flushed, reclaimed

166

it again to wipe at her eyes. "No, it isn't that. I do miss Swann, but . . . but it's been several years. It's only that . . . I didn't dare to dream. Not of something—someone—so perfect."

Perfect? Hardly—as Lightbourne and Mariah had helped him to see. But they'd taught him something else too.

He claimed her hand, raised it to his lips, and let a kiss linger on her gloved knuckles. "I rather hope you *do* dare to dream. For the first time, I want to. It would be all the sweeter if you'd share the dreams with me."

It took one more pulse, one more breath, but then her lips rose in a beautiful smile. She squeezed his fingers. "Let's dream, then. Together."

"Together." He pulled her toward the wood, out of the range of the mouselings rushing them, snowballs in hand, clearly trying to redirect them. Laughter filled his throat.

Oh yes, they would have quite the story to tell someday. He could only imagine how Emil would laugh.

*C*yril closed the doors behind the last of the audience members being shooed out the door and the few remaining helpers who would now dash to join their friends and relatives in the wood. The mice would use snowballs and acorns to redirect them, and the heroic characters would guide toward the generally correct areas with songs and dancing.

He slipped over to Mariah's side, grinning when he saw what she did—Gyldenkrone and Louise, arm in arm, paying more attention to each other than to the path the little mice were chasing them toward. "I don't think he needed our help."

She shook her head good-naturedly. "Well, one could never accuse the greve of not knowing his own mind. Or of being too shy to act on it. It seems he realized the obvious too, and so why delay?"

"Good." Cyril jauntily offered his own arm. "Now. Shall we?"

She took his arm, and he led her skipping through the snow-covered garden, aimed not for the Almond Gate, but for the more direct route to the lake. They had to be there to receive whoever found the gold-paper–wrapped box and brought it to the sleighs that ought to be lined up and waiting.

They were only halfway there when a snowball exploded against

Cyril's back. "Hey!" It was more a laugh than a shout, but he spun to see who the culprit was.

One of the Green boys, though he didn't remember the right name just yet. The lad's eyes went wide with alarm but quickly melted its way into laughter and then apology. "Sorry, Mr. Light-bourne, Lady Mariah. Didn't realize who you were."

Mariah chuckled. "Good to know you're doing your job so enthusiastically, Henry."

When he grinned, his cheeks all but vanished beneath his paper-cone nose . . . which was growing a bit soggy in the snow. "This is the best Christmas Eve ever. Can we do it next year? Or do *something* that lets me throw snowballs at the blokes?"

They both laughed, and Cyril said, "I'm with young Mr. Green. I think a village-wide holiday play is a perfect new tradition. We ought to start writing next year's while the Christmas spirit is still upon us, my lady. That will give us plenty of time to prepare."

"Yeah!" That pronouncement apparently enough of a promise for him, the little mouse scurried off, scooping up more snow for a new snowball on his way.

Mariah, still grinning, turned them back toward their shortcut. "It came together rather well, didn't it?"

"Indeed. When everyone works together, amazing things can happen. A good life lesson, I think." Certainly a good one for a future landlord. He hoped he'd always remember it—how all it had taken to unite this whole community was the promise of joy and hope and the humble asking for help.

Perhaps he ought to take a lesson from Gyldenkrone and start a journal. To make certain he never forgot such lessons.

"Though we can't just have the children's play as our lead-in to the treasure hunt every year. They ought to have the chance to hunt for the prize too." She flashed him a grin, her cheeks and nose prettily pink from the chill. "Especially since we can reuse the prize every year."

"Stroke of genius, that," Cyril agreed. "Glad the professor thought of it."

"I only hope the snow doesn't cover it over. We don't want to lose it—can you imagine?"

He chuckled. "I daresay the wood will provide enough shelter. The snow won't be quite as thick in there, at least not yet. And we found a good spot for it."

"And I suppose if the hour grows too late and no one has found it, we'll give them hint upon hint until someone does."

"I will be utterly surprised if it comes to that."

They could hear the hunt, though from here he only caught stray glimpses of color through the trunks of the trees. Laughter rang out merrily, along with squeals. And the occasional thunk of a snowball finding its target.

No one had made it to the lake yet, happily. Well, no one but the two they'd arranged to meet them there. Kellie and Blakely stood in front of the sleighs, talking and laughing. Mariah's maid spotted them first and directed Kellie's attention toward them with a smile while she reached into one of the sleighs and pulled out a bundle of fabric.

"This part was a stroke of genius too," Mariah said, giving him a smile so warm it was a wonder the snow didn't melt.

He shrugged off the compliment but not the smile. "Didn't seem quite fair that we wouldn't have some role in our own story."

When they'd written it as children, Mariah had lobbied to have the story end when their little heroine had grown up—the prince must return for her, she declared, and marry her so that they could live happily ever after.

It had been one of their many arguments. What did Cyril care, after all, about that? Growing up and taking on the responsibility it entailed hadn't sounded like a perfect ending to him. He'd insisted they end their story while the girl and the nutcracker-turned-human were still young. Still able to live in their imaginations.

But she'd been right, of course. The real world always found them, whether they wanted it to or not. Their part, then, ought to be to bring what magic they could into the world with them. Steal a bit of the joy of childhood and carry it always in their pockets—or their hearts, as it were.

Would she still want the fairy prince to carry her away? Or in this case, to stay here with him forever? Would she grant him a chance to be that prince?

He'd know soon.

Kellie greeted him with a smile and the old military jacket they'd dug up from the attic, which looked close enough to the nutcracker's style. "Found the hat too," he pronounced happily, waving it in the air. "You'll be quite the grand hussar."

"Perfect." Cyril shrugged off his cape coat and traded it for the uniform, doing the same with his hat a moment later. "How do I look?"

"Dashing." With a grin, Kellie pulled a promising little paper bag from the floor of the sleigh too. "And here. Mrs. Trutchen insisted you'd need a little something to tide you over out here in the cold."

With a grin of his own, Cyril took the bag and, after a gentle squeeze to ascertain what was in it, tucked it into his pocket. Sugar plums, naturally. Perfect. He didn't want to sample one now—with his luck, he'd have a mouth full of the chewy confection just as the winners rushed forth with their treasure in hand—but he'd share them with Mariah after they'd ushered the players into their sleighs.

He spun to see how her own transformation was going, and his eyes went wide. Like his own, her impromptu costume was more outerwear than anything. But she or her maid had dug up a cloak of thick, luxurious velvet in deep purple, trimmed in white fur and embroidered with silver and gold thread.

"What queen did you borrow that from?" he had to ask.

She laughed and spun in a quick circle so that it flowed out around her. "It was Papa's mother's, I believe. Or stored with her things, anyway. Magnificent, isn't it?"

"And instead of your hat, my lady . . ." Blakely held out a box with a grin. "Found this with the late countess's things too. His lordship said you were welcome to wear it tonight. I think he thought I meant for the ball, but why not start now?"

Clearly intrigued, Mariah pulled the lid off the short, square box and then gasped at whatever was inside.

A tiara, he saw a second later as she reached in almost reverently and pulled it out. Not an uncommon thing for a countess to have, he supposed. Even having missed the London Season, he'd seen enough drawings and photographs in newspapers to know that such accessories were a favorite for noblewomen to wear to balls.

This one shimmered with gold and was inlaid with purple stones he guessed were amethyst—though why a tiara with so many gemstones had been in a random corner of the attic and not in the earl's safe with, presumably, the other family jewels, he couldn't imagine.

Perhaps Mariah heard his thoughts. "It's paste. The late countess had duplicates made of her grand pieces, which she would wear in place of the real ones on most occasions. She had a necklace stolen once and became quite paranoid. But it's just as lovely, isn't it? I always loved this purple one." She touched a finger to one of the large oval stones. "Don't they put you in mind of plums?"

"Perfect, then, for the lady of Sugar Plum Manor."

She grinned at him, unfastened her hat, and let Blakely position the tiara on her hair. Snow quickly claimed the newly available space too, but the crystals clung for only a moment before melting. Even so, she looked as if she really had just stepped from a fairy tale.

Blakely clapped her hands together, beaming. "Absolute perfection. And with that, Kellie and I had better hurry back to the house so that everything's ready for you when you come in. Don't linger too long out here, now—you do still have a ball to dress for."

"I know, I know." Mariah touched a hand to the tiara. "This will go with the gown too, don't you think?"

"Beautifully." That assurance given, Blakely moved to Kellie's side, and the two set off for the house with waves and demands for a full update on how the adventure ended.

Cyril could turn his full focus, then, on Mariah. He offered his arm once more. "Ready to greet our guests, princess?"

She chuckled and rested her hand on his forearm in a far more stiff and formal way than usual, and they turned to face the exit from the wood, set off for the adventurers with velvet ropes someone had dug up from a nearby theater. The laughter and shouts from within the forest had grown a bit louder.

Mariah's face softened. "I admit it—I was afraid my family would think this . . . silly. Stupid. I can't say how relieved I am that they seem to be enjoying themselves."

"As am I." Not because he feared being deemed silly or even stupid by the family—but because embracing this joy meant embracing hope, embracing light. And it was a relief to know they could. That they were willing to. How dismal life would be without that.

Other words, more important words, warmed on his tongue, ready to be spoken. But he didn't dare, not yet. Not when at any moment the household could come bursting out of the tree line. No, much like the sugar plums, his heart would have to keep a few minutes more.

But only a few. The snow must not have hidden the package too much, because soon enough, Fred came dancing out, the small golden box held high as Castleton tried, laughing, to reach up and snatch it from him.

Mariah's breath of laugh sounded incredulous. "Is that Fred? Acting like a child? Teasing Papa?"

"Either that or we're sharing a vision of madness."

But it really was Fred, cheeks pink, hat covered in snow, and smiling—truly smiling—in a way Cyril had yet to see him do. He was flaunting his victory, yes, but with nothing but teasing in his tone as he mocked his parents for being too slow.

His shouts of success must have urged the others to cut short the hunt and follow the path, because after those first three came a steady stream of family and staff, all emerging from the trees with smiles and laughter. They came in twos and threes and fours, arms linked together, hands sometimes clasped in hands, shoulders touching.

Cyril drew in a long, happy breath. It had turned out exactly as Mariah had hoped. A snatch of adventure, a dose of fun, a dash of competition for a mystery prize. It had united them. More, it had filled them with joy and anticipation. It had made their hearts and faces bright.

He couldn't think of a more fitting way to usher in this holy night. The Christ child they would celebrate had already touched each of them with His love. And He'd done it through the sweet imagination of the woman beside him.

Please, Lord, he prayed even as the happy crowd approached. *Please help me to keep her always beside me. Nothing in this world would make me happier.*

Fred reached them first, though only by a few steps. His eyes glimmered with a lightness Cyril had never seen in them, and he was grinning wide as he held out the golden box with its white ribbon, still tied. The expression took about a decade from his looks. He could have been a boy with a mouse nose tied to his face and a rope tail dangling behind him.

More fascinating still, he took one look at Cyril and his sister and dropped to one knee, holding up the box as if it were his pledge of fealty. "My lord nutcracker, my princess. I have recovered the golden box and present it to you as instructed."

Mariah's lips twitched. If he was surprised to see her brother playing along so fully, he could only imagine how she felt. She'd said he'd been like this once, eager to join her games of make-believe. But not for many years. Since he went off to school. Since the burden of the Lyons estate and title loomed and then rested so heavily on his shoulders.

"Well done, brave knight," she said, projecting her voice enough that it would reach the rest of the crowd too. Their happy chatter faded as they realized she was speaking. "Well done, all! Your laughter has unlocked the magic of Christmas Wood, and your joy has sent the vile mouse king, Squeaks, away from our kingdom for good! For his treachery cannot stand in the face of such joy and goodness. And as long as peace reigns in your hearts and on your lips, he will remain banished."

"But beware!" Cyril added on cue. "When strife comes among you, so will Squeaks and his minions. Cling to the joy, my loyal subjects. Cling to the love warming your hearts now as you prepare to celebrate the true King."

"Hasten now to prepare for this grand celebration! Sir Frederick the Brave, bring your prize to the ball with you, and you will see what magic it unleashes."

They stepped to the side, indicating that the guests should pile into the sleighs. Fred, however, moved to his sister first and gave her a swift hug. "This was fun, Ri," he said. "Just what I didn't know I needed."

Within a few minutes, everyone had climbed into the line of sleighs—Fred and the Castletons and their personal servants in the first, Gyldenkrone and Louise and some other upper staff in the second, and so on. And then they were dashing toward the manor, bells jingling merrily on the horses' harnesses and laughter filling the air once again.

Beside him, Mariah let out a happy sigh. "Better even than I imagined. And that Fred found it!" She laughed in delight. "I honestly expected him to be moping at the back of the pack, furious at being dragged into the game."

He caught her hand in his and gave it a squeeze. "Those least likely to want a bit of fun are the ones most in need of it. I'm glad he embraced it."

"Me too. And now I suppose we had better walk back." But she didn't take off, plowing new tracks through the snow already filling their old ones.

Good. Had she tried it, he would have had to stop her. As it was, he could shift to move in front of her and reach for her other hand too. "Mariah, I . . . Before we go in, I have a confession to make."

Though she frowned, it couldn't erase the joy shining from her whole self. "That sounds terribly serious."

"Serious, yes. But happy, I hope." He lifted their joined hands between them, easing closer. "I'm afraid I lied. Last week, when I arrived."

"Lied." That probably sounded quite serious to her ears. Her brows sank lower.

He nodded. "I lied when I said that I was happy with your suggestion that we just be friends. I'm afraid . . . I'm afraid it didn't take but an hour for me to regret agreeing to that."

Now her brows flew upward. And he hoped with everything in him that the shift of her expression from lighthearted to something deeper was because it was wonder that filled her, and not dread. It didn't *look* like dread, but she didn't say anything.

He lifted her hands higher and pressed a kiss to each set of knuckles. "Mariah—my lady. My princess. I have no desire to imagine a future without you at my side. Please tell me you'll let me try to win your heart. Give me a chance to be more than your old friend."

It wasn't just the laughter that rang out like silver bells that made his heart sing—it was the sheen of happy tears in her eyes and the way she leaned closer too. "Silly Cyril. You needn't try to win my heart. It's been yours all these years. There is no one I would rather serve beside to make our little corner of the world filled with joy and love."

Love. A week ago, as he was preparing to leave London and come here, he'd thought the whole notion one that brought more pain than joy. But that was only because he'd let himself forget.

Let himself be ruled by his fears and insecurities. Let himself think this—her—nothing but a dream.

Yet here she stood before him, promising a lifetime of laughter to counter every heartache. Of smiles to combat every pain. Of dreams to lead them through any nightmares life threw at them.

It felt as though his blood bubbled like champagne. Laughing, he let go her hands so he could put his own on her waist, lift her, spin her around in the whirl of Christmas snow. When he put her feet on the ground again, she was laughing too, and she made no argument when he drew her closer, his arms wrapped now around her.

He caught her gaze and lowered his head, asking silently if this could possibly be true. If she'd let him kiss her, let him clasp hold of this dream.

She circled her arms around his neck and tilted her face up to meet his. Answer enough for him. He touched his lips to hers— and he could have sworn he heard a chorus of angels singing. Or perhaps that was just the echo of the neighbors singing a carol as they trekked back toward their homes.

Either way. He kissed her softly, a promise of what was to come. And then again, because he couldn't help himself. More, because she was the sweetest thing he'd ever tasted.

When he pulled away enough to claim a breath, she smiled up at him again, her eyes looking as dazed as he felt. "Please tell me you're not planning a long and drawn-out courtship with an equally long and drawn-out engagement. Are you?"

Was he? It was probably the reasonable thing. But then, her parents had been willing to let her go off with Gyldenkrone to Denmark after scarcely an introduction. Cyril, at least, would be here, right here, all the time. Even with four years of near-silence and twelve since they'd last been face-to-face, they knew each other so well.

"Perish the thought." Perhaps they would need a bit of length to their engagement—there were plans to be made, after all, and put into reality. But they both knew what they wanted. He dropped to one knee, claiming her hands again. He didn't have a ring—didn't honestly even know how to get one. But he had something to offer, anyway.

Grinning, he withdrew the bag of sugar plums and pulled one out, held it up. "It's the only sparkling thing I have to offer right now. But I think it's a fine symbol of all I would make yours. Will you marry me, Lady Mariah Lyons? Will you spend your life here with me at Plumford? At Sugar Plum Manor?"

She took the plum from his fingers, the most beautiful smile in the world on her lips. "Yes and yes and yet another yes. Today, tomorrow, and forever."

What was he to do but surge to his feet and seal the promise with another kiss?

16

Mariah stood at the entrance to the ballroom, her smile so perpetual that her cheeks ached. She couldn't have let it fall from her lips had she tried. How could she? Today, at least, life was perfect. She stood beside her papa and Cyril—her betrothed!—in front of the cart full of sweets and candies. She handed a bag of sugar plums and marzipan and other delights to each of the children, wishing them a Happy Christmas.

Music danced through the air from the string quartet set up between the Christmas tree and Skylark's castle, still cloaked. A thousand lights twinkled from tree limbs and chandeliers and the fire in the hearth. It was Christmas. And it was the happiest day of her life. Because she had this family and these people and the man she'd loved since they were children beaming at her side as if he'd just been handed the keys to a kingdom.

Papa intercepted her gaze when there was a momentary lull in the receiving line, sending her a wink. He and Mama had been waiting for them when she and Cyril arrived back at the house two hours ago to thank her for bringing the play they'd missed to them, congratulate them on such a clever and fun adventure—and to share that Louise and Gyldenkrone had asked for their blessing on a quick engagement. The greve wanted to take Louise back to Denmark with him as his fiancée and introduce her to his family, and Louise had been thrilled.

Perhaps they'd been afraid the news would upset Mariah, but she'd put that to rest within seconds, first rejoicing for her sister and then sharing her own news. It was too perfect a match for them to do anything as silly as insist on a long courtship, but they had recommended a Christmas wedding next year, no doubt to give her and Cyril plenty of time to be certain they were certain.

On the one hand, waiting a year seemed torturous. On the other hand, it would be a year of joy as they got reacquainted with every detail about each other. And a Christmas wedding! She couldn't think of anything better. Marrying at the chapel at Plumford would always be a delight . . . but marrying at the chapel at Sugar Plum Manor would be magical.

And now here she stood, knowing that here she would stand for every Christmas for the rest of her life. Well, unless they took one to visit Louise and Gyldenkrone in Denmark some year. She didn't want to miss their own ball, but the Dane had regaled them with tales of his country's traditions while they waited for the guests to arrive, and it did sound charming. She'd like to experience it someday, so long as Cyril was by her side as her husband.

That was for some future time, though. For now, this. Her favorite night of the year. The glee of each child who entered, who took their beautifully made candies with such enthusiasm, and who rushed then to the tree, where Professor Skylark gave them each their special nutcracker gift. The rainbow of gorgeous gowns twirling about as the couples danced. The laughter. The music. The peace. The joy.

Cyril took her hand in his as the last of the guests filtered in. "You," he whispered into her ear, "are the most beautiful woman at any ball ever. My princess."

Papa had drifted away in conversation with Mr. Nithercott, so Mariah had no compunction in turning to her beloved with a smile that must look every bit as besotted as she felt. "And you are the most handsome prince."

He looked at her in the same way he'd done just before he kissed her. Of course, he couldn't repeat that just now, but he would sometime. And she thrilled at the thought. She knew that life wouldn't be all moments like this—but she thanked the Lord for this one.

He bowed before her, rising again with a smile. "May I have this dance, my lady?"

"With pleasure."

She'd attended this ball since she was one of the children, had danced countless times at it with nearly every fellow in the room— her father, her brother, their more extended family, the neighbors from both Castleton and Hope, and those from the wider county who wanted to join them. But no dance had ever been like this dance, in the arms of the man she'd spend her life with. Never had she felt more the princess than she did now with her new gown, commissioned to impress a Danish lord who had so wisely chosen her sister instead, with a tiara of glittering Sugar Plum amethysts—or so she'd dubbed them—on her head.

Papa had taken one look at the paste version from the attic and declared she ought to wear the real one tonight, when they were celebrating two engagements as well as the coming of the King of Kings. He'd taken Cyril with him to the safe that held the Castleton jewels, and they'd returned with more than just the headpiece. Cyril had a matching amethyst ring too, its purple oval surrounded by diamonds. And he'd slid it onto her finger with a promise of what was to come.

She didn't think her feet actually touched the floor all through this, their first dance as a couple.

The music came to a halt after the waltz ended, and Mariah gripped Cyril's arm, excitement zinging through her. "It's time," she whispered. "The unveiling."

Cyril chuckled. "You've already seen it, you know."

"But not moving. And I haven't seen them see it." She motioned to the crowd of children clamoring around the covered castle, bouncing on their toes in anticipation.

Cyril led her to the edge of the room, where they had a good view but weren't in the way of the children.

Professor Skylark had taken his spot, much as he'd done for the family the other night. But his smile was always at its brightest when he was with children. He spoke to them a moment, asking them what they hoped was beneath the cover—getting answers as varied as the answerers. He asked if they'd been good boys and girls this year. And then, when their impatience was at its peak, he grabbed hold of the edge of the silken cover and gave it a tug.

It rippled down, revealing the castle beneath. Even having studied it before, Mariah still had to gasp in awe. The lights from the Christmas tree twinkled in its tiny windows, and it looked different to her, knowing it was about to come alive.

The professor scanned the room. "Lord Lyons? Time for your prize to shine. I do hope you brought it with you."

Fred edged his way through the crowd, his wide smile warming a whole different part of her heart. It had been fifteen years since she'd seen him smile like that. Fifteen years since he'd just been Fred, her brother, and not Lord Lyons. Or no. He'd been Lord Lyons then too—he just hadn't fully realized it yet. Now, it seemed he'd reclaimed a sliver of that boyhood good humor. And she prayed with everything in her that he'd hold onto it.

He held up the golden box and then, with a flourish, untied the white bow and let the ribbon slip away. Unwrapped the paper, lifted the lid, and brandished what it had been hiding.

A small silver key.

He'd probably guessed by now what his prize was, but that would make it no less a treasure. The professor had never, not once, let anyone but himself turn on the magic of his creation. That he'd offered it as a special gift today was no small thing. And given the many times Fred had tried to wheedle him into sharing the honor, it was especially fun that he'd been the one to find it.

Professor Skylark smiled, nodded, and indicated the place hidden in the castle's base where the key would fit. "Very good then, my lord. Insert the key and twist clockwise until it stops."

As Fred twisted, the sound of winding gears ticked from the castle. With each additional click, another notch in their own anticipation grew. When finally it stopped, Skylark indicated the switch beside the key, and Fred, catching his breath first and looking up to meet her gaze, smiled and flicked.

The castle sprang to life. Windows and doors opened and closed, the figures that had been installed on their tracks the other night began gliding through their courses, and music unlike any she'd ever heard tinkled out.

She spotted the figure she'd chosen as the hero, dancing with a dark-haired girl in a purple gown, and she smiled. Then she laughed when the other figure burst from another door, his wooden arms raised as if they were on the attack. His appearance sent the other two scattering, though their tracks eventually circled back together. The villain slipped back into his door, and the dance repeated.

She took in the other little mechanical miracles too—the children who slid down the snowy hill and then climbed back up it; the little dog chasing a postman along a narrow street; the flock of birds on thread-slender wires that went round and round the castle, their altitudes shifting as they flew; the carolers that sang at one door, bowed, and moved to the next.

For a quarter of an hour, it held them rapt as they watched each of the mechanical stories play out. But then, as always happened, they learned all the stories, and the children began drifting away, back to the toys they could make move according to their own desires and the treats still waiting to be eaten. The adults returned to their dancing and talking, sipping and nibbling.

Mariah stayed, though, and Cyril with her. More surprising,

Louise and Fred both joined her too, and Gyldenkrone with them. They stood for a long moment more, watching the magic of Professor Skylark's imagination played out in synchronized clockworks.

Louise grasped Mariah's hand. "Well, little sister," she said, contentment making her voice richer than ever, "I don't know how you've done it. But you've delivered everyone a happily-ever-after this Christmas."

Mariah smiled but shook her head. "No. It wasn't my doing— that's the thing. It was everyone coming together that made it possible. That's where joy is always found."

"True." Louise leaned over, bumping their shoulders together. "But sometimes . . . sometimes we need a bit of help to see it."

Sometimes they did. And if she could be the one, now and then, to deliver that help, then she would count it as the deepest honor. She would bring any joy she could to whomever the Lord put in her path.

She and Cyril, their family and friends . . . and all who crossed through the Almond Gate and into the heart of Sugar Plum Manor. Here, she prayed, they would always find the heart of Christmas waiting to welcome them home.

Author's Note

Since my daughter was five and first joined our local ballet troupe, *The Nutcracker* has been a part of our lives. As Xoë grew from sweet little girl into beautiful teenager, her roles in the ballet changed and grew too. One of our favorite moments each year was seeing which party dress she would get to wear and which new fairy dances she'd get to learn. Tchaikovsky's gorgeous music has been listened and danced to so many times in our lives that we know it by heart . . . and Christmas isn't Christmas around here without its familiar strains.

So, when my amazing editor at Bethany House (thank you, Rochelle!) asked if I'd have any interest in writing a short Christmas novel, I quickly proposed something *Nutcracker*-inspired. It didn't take me long to decide that I'd prefer to base the actual story, though, not on the ballet, which was itself an adaptation, but on the original story by E. T. A. Hoffman. Written for children, his little book had the backstory of why the nutcracker prince and the mouse king were at war, and more adventure in its pages. It also ends in reality rather than in the dreamworld, with the lovely Marie all grown up and the handsome prince coming to claim her as his bride.

In my version, I obviously made countless changes, but I so enjoyed the shout-outs to the original, from my character names to the play they put on, from the designations of the fairyland locations to the treats and candies. And of course I needed a clever clockmaker. No one knows what *Drosselmeier* actually means, but some think part of the name is taken from a German songbird, and so I named my professor after an *English* songbird, the skylark.

A quick note on sugar plums themselves. There is, in fact, a traditional treat that is made as I describe here, with preserved plums or prunes, baked over and over again and rolled in sugar (you can find a recipe on my website). A Byzantine variation involves mincing the fruit and combining it with nuts and rolling the balls in sugar—easier by far, though a different consistency. These treats were so popular that *sugar plum* became a name for *any* candy, especially at Christmas. My story pays homage to the original.

Most of all, I wanted this tale to be one of wonder, one that captures the joy of Christmas that children always feel and that adults too often forget. I wanted to capture, as Hoffman did in his original story, how crucial it is to keep hold of that wonder. Because what could be more wondrous than the reminder that our God took on human flesh and came to earth to save us? He is the source of all joy. And He not only entrusts it to us, He trusts us to extend it to others.

If you'd like a peek into the original magic world of Hoffman and my own adaptation, I hope you'll visit my website at RoseannaM White.com/SugarPlumManor.

I wish you all the happiest of Christmases and joy in the months and years to come!

Plum Kringle

For the crust

2 cups flour
3 tablespoons sugar
2 teaspoons instant yeast
1 teaspoon fine sea salt
1 cup butter, cold, cut into pieces
1/3 cup whole milk
1 large egg
1 egg white for the wash

For the filling

1 cup plum preserves

For the icing

1 cup powdered sugar
2 tablespoons milk
1 teaspoon vanilla

Combine the flour, sugar, yeast, and salt in a large bowl and mix. Add the butter and cut together, either with a pastry cutter, two knives, or a few pulses in a food processor. You want the butter to be reduced to pea-sized pieces.

Whisk the whole egg and milk together. Add to the dry mixture and gently fold until it comes together in a dough. (If the dough is too crumbly, add a few drops of water at a time, just until it holds together when pinched.) Shape into a flattened disc, wrap in plastic, and refrigerate 6–48 hours.

On a floured work surface, roll the dough into a rectangle approximately 9x15 inches (you can mark it out on the underside of a piece of parchment paper and roll directly onto it for ease of measurement). Take the short ends of the dough and fold it into thirds, creating a 9x5 rectangle. Turn it 90 degrees and repeat the process. Wrap again and chill for another 30 minutes.

Repeat the step above. At this point, you can either make and bake the kringle, refrigerate it for up to 2 days, or freeze it for up to 3 months.

When ready to assemble, line two baking sheets with parchment paper. Divide the dough in half and roll each portion into a 5x20 rectangle. Spread a thin line of preserves down the middle of each, leaving 2 inches on either side and a half inch at the ends.

Fold one long side of dough over the jam. Use the egg white to brush over the unfolded portion and ends. Fold that over as well, pinching and smoothing the dough closed all along the side and on the ends. Form each length of dough into a circle, pinching the ends to unite. Flip them so that the seam is downward onto the parchment-lined baking sheets. Cover and let rise for 45 minutes in a warm place.

Preheat the oven to 375°. Once the oven is hot and the dough has puffed, brush the egg wash over the top and sides of the kringles and then bake for about 20 minutes or until golden brown.

Whisk powdered sugar, milk, and vanilla in a small bowl. Drizzle over the warm pastry. Remove pastry to a wire rack to cool.

Best enjoyed within a day of baking, though it will keep at room temperature for 3 to 4 days.

Recipe makes 2 pastries. Feel free to substitute any fruit or nut filling; traditional Danish kringle uses a tart cherry jam and almond paste.

For a quicker dough recipe and other treats from the book, visit RoseannaMWhite.com/recipes and scroll to the section for *Christmas at Sugar Plum Manor* recipes.

Read on

FOR A SNEAK PEEK AT

An

HONORABLE
DECEPTION

THE FINAL BOOK OF
THE IMPOSTERS SERIES.

AVAILABLE NOVEMBER 2024.

1

Fairfax House
London, England
15 August 1910

*Y*ates let the barbell clang back into its brackets and pushed up to sitting, his eyes searching for the utilitarian clock on the wall. Sweat dripped from his brow, forcing him to wipe it off before he could make sense of the time. Three in the afternoon. He had just enough time to bathe and dress before he had to get to James's church on the other side of the city for his appointment with a potential client. If he didn't roast to death in the meantime.

He moved to the open window, but the breeze that trickled through did little to cool him. London was often miserable in the summer, but today it was doing a fair imitation of the pits of the netherworld. And it would only get worse once his sister and her husband left for Northumberland tomorrow.

It was absolutely no fair that they got to escape the city while he was stuck here, sitting in Lords and voting on bills he scarcely cared about and working on Imposters business while they had their holiday at home at Fairfax Tower.

Absolutely unfair. They'd already made him suffer two months of solitude after the wedding, before they agreed to move back to the House and let Merritt's rented townhome go. It was just cruel to subject him to his own company again now.

Lionfeathers, but it was hot. He mopped his face off with a towel and charged from the room, ready to find Marigold wherever she was and let her know, yet again, what a horrible, horrible sister she was to abandon him like this and go back to the cool sea breezes and comforts of home without him. Wasn't it bad enough that she only kept him company in the gymnasium for half an hour a day lately, and then only to do the lightest, easiest of exercises?

He followed her voice to the drawing room, pausing when he caught tones that were neither hers nor Clementina's nor Gemma's—did she actually have a guest? One that would be outraged if he barged in wearing only his leotard and pajama-style trousers he wore when taking his exercise?

He listened a moment more and then relaxed. It was only Lavinia. She may be as much a lady as his own sister, being the daughter of Earl Hemming as she was, but she was also their closest neighbor in Northumberland and had seen him in every possible mode of dress over the years. He barreled through the door, perhaps with a bit more gusto than it really demanded. "Cruel creature," he pronounced upon entering, scowling at his sister.

She sat on the couch, her hair still done up in an elaborate braided coiffure, one of her magnificently ridiculous hats on the cushion beside her, and her dress looking straight from the highest of haute couture boutiques in Paris, despite having actually come from their own attic. She was setting tongues ablaze, he knew, daring to wear fashionable ensembles when she was in a delicate condition as she was.

Three more months, by the doctor's estimation, before she presented him with his first niece or nephew. He alternated between unbridled joy and unfettered panic at the thought.

Everything was going to change. Everything already had. No trapeze acts just now, no acrobatics that required two people in

192

their investigations. What's worse, she looked so blasted *tired*, and her face was pale beneath her smile.

She quirked a brow at him. "Are you still pouting about staying in London?"

"Of course I am." It was his sworn duty as her pesky little brother, after all, to complain to her. "It's hot as blazes."

She chuckled. But even that sounded tired. "So come with us."

If only he could. Were it only the Sessions, he might well choose to duck out of them—there was nothing really urgent up for vote, not that his vote mattered on, anyway. But there was still a case that needed wrapping up, and the appointment later today could well result in another. And rarely did their cases allow for investigation in their own home county.

And the last one that did had been anything but pleasant. Which reminded him to send a smile to Lavinia. "Hello, Vin."

Only when he glanced at her did he realize that she'd been looking at *him* ever since he barged in, an amused look on her face. "Yates."

Lady Lavinia Hemming was, without question, beautiful. And he could admit—to his sister, anyway—that he'd been in love with her for a good portion of his life. But that was before he realized his father had left him not so much as a tuppence with which to run the estate, before they'd had to let all their servants go and—gasp—learn to cook their own food and take on work to make ends meet. He'd known as he sat in the solicitor's office beside Marigold and heard that there was nothing left of the Fairfax fortune that Lavinia was never going to be his wife. Then she'd caught scarlet fever, had nearly died, and had been all but bedridden for years from the ensuing heart condition. While the part of him that would have liked to be her hero wanted to rally at that and think, *Ah, I can prove my eternal love!*, the fact was, he'd scarcely seen her for years. Her parents weren't exactly keen on letting an eighteen-year-old male into their eighteen-year-old daughter's bedroom, after all.

And he'd had to focus on earning them enough income to survive on.

Seven years later, he'd learned to look at her without that punch to his gut. Which was good, since she'd been courted by no fewer than a half-dozen leading gentlemen since she finally came out last year, after her recovery. Most of them just this summer, when she returned to London after the first few horrible months of grief from first learning her mother was a traitor and then mourning her death.

She wasn't exactly glowing with the societal success though. If anything, she looked as weary as Marigold, and without the handy excuse. He frowned. "You look like a stout wind could blow you over. Have you been sleeping?"

Lavinia rolled her green eyes. "Yes, Father."

"Eating?"

"*Yes.*"

"Exercising?"

At that, she let out a huff. "My physicians have cautioned me not to overexert myself. You know that."

"*Over*, yes. But a bit of exertion is necessary for regaining one's strength."

The look she sent at his arms wasn't exactly admiring. "I suppose you think yourself the expert, Mr. Strongman?"

His lips twitched upward. "That's *Lord* Strongman to you. And I'll have you know that after my devastating wound, which I took saving *your* life—"

"You did not!" It got her laughing, anyway. If they could laugh about it now, that surely meant her heart was recovering from the blow her mother had dealt it. "*I* saved *you!*"

He waved away that little detail. "While recuperating, I definitely found it of the utmost importance to push myself a little more each day, to truly recover."

Lavinia rolled her eyes. "It was barely a scratch."

"I took a dagger to the leg! Eight stitches!" But he grinned and flopped down beside her on her sofa, leaning in and draping a sweaty arm around her just to watch her flinch away and wrinkle her nose. "Come on, my lady. Join me in the gymnasium. I'll have your heart as healthy as Leonidas's in a month."

"Tempting as that is . . ." Lavinia nodded toward Marigold. "I've come today to beg your sister to let me go home with her and keep her company at the Tower until Papa decides to return to Northumberland. I've found I've had my fill of Town."

It had tired her too quickly, she meant. The late nights, the rich foods, the stress of gossip—and there had been no shortage of that. The country air would restore her, though. As would his sister's company. Yates nodded, reclaimed his arm, and pushed back to his feet. "Good. Any gents you want me to look into while you're gone?"

She didn't know about their private investigation firm, The Imposters, Ltd. But she *did* know he was a friend, and that he'd make sure anyone she was considering was deserving of her.

Lavinia shook her head. "No. They're all . . . no."

Leopard stripes. There was a world of meaning in that sigh she let out that he didn't have time to explore right now. But Marigold would take care of it. He made certain of that with a glance her way, and then moved toward the door. "Well, I know you two will cry over it, but I have an appointment to keep. Enjoy your trip north tomorrow. Know you have my envy."

Their laughter followed as he vaulted up the stairs, and he made quick work of his ablutions so that he could slide down the banister again and hurry out the door.

Hot, damp air swamped him the moment he stepped outside. The thermometer read ninety-five degrees, but the dratted uniform of the gentry—shirt, waistcoat, tie, jacket—made it feel about twice that. What he wouldn't give to be able to leave the house in his exercise garb.

Usually he'd walk to a tube station farther from home just to stretch his legs, but today he opted for the underground as quickly as possible, and he thanked the good Lord for the coolness of the cavernous cathedral when he stepped inside its back door twenty minutes later. Voices from James's office said he must be with a parishioner, which was too bad—Yates always enjoyed popping in and chatting with their former steward's son whenever he could. James didn't know *precisely* what they did, just that they did it. He knew why, and he knew they focused on truth and justice, so he lent them the old confessional for their meetings whenever Yates needed it.

He slipped into the confessor's side of the booth, indulging in a long breath and loosening of his necktie. Though he pulled a slender tome of poetry from his pocket, he didn't open it yet. He closed his eyes. He breathed out a prayer. And he looked deep into himself.

Ever since he started meeting potential clients in this booth, he'd made a habit of examining his own conscience first. To make certain he was always working for the Good, that he didn't fall into judgment as he investigated truths that were too often ugly. And to ensure that though every other foundation he ever took for granted shook, his faith didn't.

Today, he looked back over his life of the past week and had to purse his lips. Had his complaining moved from joking to true? Probably. And Gemma hadn't taken it well when he jested about how she seemed bent on catching Marigold up with the size of her stomach, though her own pregnancy was a month behind—he ought to apologize for that. He'd fallen into worry again on Friday when he was reviewing their accounts, which he knew was a lack of trust in God's provision.

And they weren't doing *badly*. They just weren't doing as well as he'd hoped they'd be. Cases always slowed down as the weather cooled and society left London for their country homes, and he'd hoped to have a bit more of a cushion for the winter this year, what with his sister and Gemma both with child. What if they needed a doctor? Hospital? Medicine?

He gave that again to the Lord, and said a prayer, while he was at it, for the health of both mothers and babies. For his sister especially . . . but then for Gemma especially. She and Graham had already lost Jamie when he was only nine months old. If anything were to happen to this babe—it didn't bear thinking about.

Another few minutes of prayer, and then he cracked open his Tennyson and read until he heard the large front doors squeak open. He glanced at his watch. The potential client—who had signed the note the urchins had delivered to him simply as *A. B.* Not exactly a lot to go on, that, but the hand had been feminine.

Not exactly *unusual*. But not the most common. The cards he placed at the Marlborough brought far more clients their way than the ones his sister and Gemma left at the ladies' clubs—a fact which he rubbed their noses in regularly, out of brotherly duty. And when women *did* hire them, all too often it was to investigate a spouse they suspected of infidelity. Not his favorite task—because far too often they proved exactly what the ladies feared.

He didn't know if he had another such investigation in him when he wouldn't have Marigold on hand to joke with and help him keep his spirits up. But then, winter was coming, and he'd just as soon it not be too lean.

The steps were definitely feminine—but quick. He heard a few moments of hesitation as the woman searched the massive chamber for the confessional, but once she spotted it, her stride became as sure as it was fast. The door to the penitent's side opened, shut again, and someone sat on the bench, nothing but a vaguely girlish silhouette through the screen. "We are such stuff . . ." she said, as he'd instructed her to.

Yates smiled and pulled forward the accent he'd decided on today—a Scottish burr. ". . . as dreams are made of. Good day . . . miss?"

Her voice sounded young—not childish, but certainly not matronly. Were he to guess, he'd have put her somewhere in the general range of his own twenty-three years, give or take a few. But he'd found it always wisest to err on the side of youth when addressing women he didn't know. Give a *madame* to the wrong one and you'd earn quite a scowl.

"Miss will suffice. Miss B."

His lips twitched. A cagey one, then. He could understand that, on the one hand. But if she really thought she could hire a P.I. without her own identity becoming known, she was in for a surprise. "All right then. Mr. A. How can I help you today, Miss B?"

The woman drew in a deep breath and let it slowly out. "I would like to hire you to find someone."

He frowned. The last time they'd been hired to find someone, it had been a kidnapped boy, and it had turned challenging in a hurry. "Missing person?"

"Not . . . exactly. At least, I don't know that she is. Everyone says she isn't. Except she *is*."

"Uh huh." That clarified things. Yates leaned back against the wall of the booth, imagining himself a Scottish laird of centuries gone by. "I'd love to say I ken what you mean, Miss B, but a bit more information wouldn't go awry, aye?"

Another sigh. "All right. It's my ayah, from when I was a girl."

Yates sat up again, his brows furrowing even though his guest wouldn't see it. "You grew up in India?"

"I did, yes, until I was twelve. When we came back to England, my childhood ayah opted to travel with us, rather than my parents hiring a stranger for the task. She left us once we reached London, of course, but she hired on with another family returning to India. I believe at this point she's made the journey five or six times, round trip."

Not uncommon, he knew. Families coming from India were happy to hire cheap nannies to keep track of their children on the journey, but rarely were they interested in keeping such unfashionable help while they were in England. And if the women couldn't find journeys home, they were often left to fend for themselves in London. It had been enough of a problem a decade or two ago that charities had sprung up to house them and manage funding to send them to and from England.

This was the first he'd heard of a grown child wanting to find her ayah again though. "And . . . you wish to reconnect? After how many years?" He'd have to determine if the woman was even in England, or back in India, or somewhere on a steamer in between.

"It isn't like that." Her words came out in a snap, then she sucked in a breath. "Forgive me. My parents . . . wouldn't exactly encourage this search."

Unmarried then, most likely, if she was worrying with her parents' opinion more than her husband's. He hadn't been willing to accept as much just by the "Miss B" bit. "No forgiveness necessary. But if you could answer the question?"

"We've kept in touch all along. Whenever she's back in London, I've managed to visit her. Only, this last time, when I went to the Ayah's Home, she wasn't there. Or so they said. Even though it's the one she said she'd be at. I've visited the others, too, and no one reports seeing her. It isn't exactly something I can take to the police, though, is it?"

"Mm. I see your point." Scotland Yard rarely wanted to bother with transients from India, especially when all they'd have to go on was one young lady's concern. "Aye, then. What can you tell me about her?"

"She's thirty years old—"

"Only thirty?" He couldn't keep the surprise from his tone. Even if Miss B was only eighteen, that would have been six years since her first transit, which would have put the nanny in her early-to-mid-twenties when she worked for the B family. Unusual indeed. Most ayahs were middle aged or older.

"She is only eight years my elder—it was why we were so close." Defensiveness colored her tone, yes. And something more.

Fear. Genuine, heartbroken fear.

Noted. This wasn't idle curiosity. This was a young woman seeking one of her dearest friends. He nodded. "Go on."

"I went to the Ayah's Home on Mare Street, in Hackney, first. That's where she always went. But when I got there, they—"

The front doors creaked open again—but not just a creak. They banged against the wall, startling Yates off his bench. Doors that size didn't just swing about in a breeze like a bedroom door at the Tower. To hit the wall with such force, they'd have had to be thrown with considerable force.

Footsteps—at least three sets of them. Heavy. Running.

Lionfeathers. What was going on? He held his breath, knowing that no one ever really thought to look in the old, abandoned confessional if they were searching for someone. If hiding were necessary, this was the best place to do it.

Though James was just back the hall in his office, and a parishioner with him. Was *he* in danger? Yates sent a prayer heavenward.

Miss B apparently didn't work through his same logic. She drew in a startled breath, and he saw her lurch toward her door.

No! He didn't dare scream it, though he willed it at her as loudly as he could, and reached toward the screen separating them.

Too late, of course. She was already out, already screaming, "You!"

Yates clenched his teeth, his hands, and tried to peer through the grate without giving himself away. He couldn't just burst out to see what was going on—he had no disguise on, and no one could know that Mr. A of the Imposters was in fact Lord Yates Fairfax, ninth Earl Fairfax. Anonymity was the key to their entire success.

Which mattered for exactly three more seconds. And then the unthinkable sounded—gunshots, there in James's church.

The next moments were a blur. He burst out, but only in time to see three men running for the doors again. He made note of their relative heights, their clothing, the color of hair he could just make out under their hats, but he didn't run after them—not given the moan from the floor.

He fell to his knees beside the young woman. Her eyes were closed, blood staining her clothes in three places. He checked for her pulse as he noted more footsteps coming from the direction of the office, found it present, and took stock the wounds.

One in her shoulder—through and through. One in her side—he prayed it had missed any vital organs. One in her leg. Whoever those men had been, they either had lousy aim or hadn't meant to kill her, only to wound her.

"Yates!"

"Blast it, James." His friend knew better than to call him by name in the presence of a client. But then, he was under duress, understandably. And Yates was out here in the open, face undisguised, so what did it matter? Besides, the girl was unconscious, despite that the gunshots shouldn't have made her so. He'd need to examine her head, see if she'd struck it on the stone of the floor as she fell. "I'm fine. It's the girl."

He looked down at her again, and recognition hit him—twice. First, the recognition that she was beautiful—beyond beautiful. And second, that it was a thought he'd had about her before—when he'd seen her in the society columns, next to photographs of his sister.

She wasn't *Miss* anything. She was Lady Alethia Barremore, daughter of the previous Viceroy of India.

And if she opened her eyes, she'd know his deepest secret.

Roseanna M. White is a bestselling, Christy Award–winning author who has long claimed that words are the air she breathes. When not writing fiction, she's homeschooling, editing, designing book covers, and pretending her house will clean itself. Roseanna is the author of a slew of historical novels that span several continents and thousands of years. Spies and war and mayhem always seem to find their way into her books . . . to offset her real life, which is blessedly ordinary. You can learn more about her and her stories at RoseannaMWhite.com.

Sign Up for Roseanna's Newsletter

Keep up to date with Roseanna's latest news on book releases and events by signing up for her email list at the link below.

RoseannaMWhite.com

FOLLOW ROSEANNA ON SOCIAL MEDIA

Roseanna M. White   @RoseannaMWhite   @RoseannaMWhite

More from Roseanna M. White

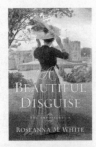

Dire straits force Lady Marigold Fairfax and her brother to become private investigators in London. When Sir Merritt Livingstone hires them to look into the father of Marigold's best friend for suspected international espionage, she is determined to discover the truth—and even more determined to keep her heart from getting involved.

A Beautiful Disguise
THE IMPOSTERS #1

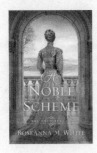

As part of England's most elite private investigation firm, Gemma and Graham must set aside their broken relationship to work together on a new case. Graham is determined to use this opportunity to win back the only woman he's ever loved, but there's no guarantee Gemma's shattered heart can be restored.

A Noble Scheme
THE IMPOSTERS #2

Lord Yates Fairfax, leader of the secretive Imposters, is pulled into a mysterious case by the beautiful Lady Alethia. Joined by one of his oldest friends, Lady Lavinia, their investigations reveal society's darkest secrets, forcing them to confront the unsettling reality that the gentry isn't always noble, and truth isn't always honorable.

An Honorable Deception
THE IMPOSTERS #3

BETHANYHOUSE

 Bethany House Fiction

 @BethanyHouseFiction

 @Bethany_House

 @BethanyHouseFiction

 Free exclusive resources for your book group at BethanyHouseOpenBook.com

 Sign up for our fiction newsletter today at BethanyHouse.com